ABEL'S
DAUGHTER

ABEL'S DAUGHTER

Edited, with an introduction, by Nancy A. Walker

THE RACHEL MADDUX SERIES
VOLUME 5

The University of Tennessee Press / Knoxville

Copyright © 1993 by The University of Tennessee Press / Knoxville.
All Rights Reserved. Manufactured in the United States of America.
First Edition.

The paper in this book meets the minimum requirements of the
American National Standard for Permanence of Paper for Printed
Library Materials. ∞ The binding materials have been chosen
for strength and durability.

Library of Congress Cataloging-in-Publication Data

Maddux, Rachel, 1913-1983
    The green kingdom / edited with an introduction by Nancy A. Walker.
—1st ed.
            p.   cm. — (The Rachel Maddux series : v. 5)
    ISBN 0-87049-781-2 (Cloth: alk. paper)
    I. Walker, Nancy A., 1942-   II. Title.
    III. Series: Maddux, Rachel, 1913-1983. Rachel Maddux series ; v. 4.
PS3563.A3395G73   1993
813' .54—dc20   92-26664
                                                        CIP

INTRODUCTION

For several months in 1942 and 1943, while Rachel Maddux's husband, King Baker, was stationed at Ft. Belvoir, Virginia, Rachel and King lived in the small town of Occoquan, Virginia. *Abel's Daughter*, first published in 1960, is based on Rachel Maddux's experience of Occoquan—in particular, her friendship with Saluka Fitzgerald, who is Serena Covington in the novel. Even in 1960, despite the beginnings of the civil rights movement, interracial friendships were rare; in 1942, in the South especially, they disturbed the established social order. Rigid, unquestioned segregation was the norm, to be transgressed at the risk of ostracism (for whites) or punishment (for blacks). But for Rachel Maddux it was normal to ignore or transcend such boundaries. Many years later, she summed up her philosophy of human equality in straightforward terms: "That's a pretty hard passage down that birth canal, and I figure that anyone who makes it has a right to be here."

Occoquan, renamed Chinkapink in *Abel's Daughter*, had once been a town of three thousand people, a resort town served by steamboats, but by the early 1940s its inhabitants, black and white, numbered just two hundred. Nevertheless, the town had two grocery stores, one run by whites and the other by the black Ogle Harris, the inspiration for Abel Loftis in the novel, father of Serena Covington. Just as Rachel and King elected to shop at the "colored" grocery, so Molly and Ted Demerest, the central characters in the novel, patronize Abel Loftis's store and thus meet Serena.

Neither Rachel Maddux, in her journal account of the Occoquan period, nor Molly Demerest, in the novel, is a crusader bent on righting the racial wrongs of more than a century, but each has a strong sense of morally decent behavior and a conviction that friendship overrides race. Thus when Molly, who (like Rachel Maddux) had attended but not completed medical school, learns that no nearby doctor is willing to diagnose competently Serena's illness, and that Serena cannot enter the hospital for surgery until space is available in the "colored" ward, she is outraged. Unable to change the system of racial discrimination, she moves outside it to give Serena moral support and practical assistance during her hospitalization and convalescence. Molly is less able to help a young black man who, falsely accused of stealing a watch, is jailed without benefit of attorney or trial in order for the county to have cheap labor to repair the roads.

But Molly Demerest's efforts to intercede on behalf of Chinkapink's black citizens do not go unnoticed or unrewarded. Serena tells Molly how to find running pine and cedar in the woods for Christmas decorations, and Serena's son, to whom Molly loans books, becomes devoted to her. The two most touching gifts are invisible. After Molly has written letters to Serena during her hospital stay, assuring her that her children are being cared for, Serena tells her of the bargain she has made with God: "I asked God would He give the time, every minute you spent on those letters, would He give it back to you in *inspired* writing time for your own work." (Rachel Maddux had begun writing her first novel, *The Green Kingdom*, by the time she lived in Occoquan.) The other invisible gift is initially perplexing. Not until they are leaving Chinkapink do Molly and Ted learn that the reason the black residents have avoided them in public was to protect them from recriminations from their white neighbors.

Serena Covington and the other black residents of Chinkapink know from bitter experience about such recriminations against white people who befriend them. The elderly Mrs. Emerson, who now lives alone on the edge of town, had once been a gifted musician who shared her talents by playing the piano for worship services at the black church. When she began offering piano lessons to black as well as white students, the white citizens turned against her, and she is now dependent on black residents such as Abel Loftis for survival. The scene in the novel that most clearly shows Abel's nobility of character occurs when Mrs. Emerson visits the Loftis store for a dish of ice cream, which Abel Loftis only pretends to put on her bill.

Yet as much as *Abel's Daughter* deals with the serious issues of human dignity and human cruelty, the novel also celebrates moments of transcendent joy, and it demonstrates in several instances Rachel Maddux's talent for amusing—sometimes wildly comic—writing. With World War II always in the background, making the future uncertain, the ritual of celebrating Christmas takes on major significance, and when Molly and Serena take a walk in the snowy woods to commemorate Serena's recovery, the blossoms of a rhododendron become a miracle—"not a thing for words." Sometimes a moment of wonder takes on a humorous tone. When Abel Loftis tells Molly Demerest about learning to read by memorizing the names of the products he sells, she realizes that his reading vocabulary consists primarily of nouns—"Kleenex, Paper Napkins, Wheaties, Oatmeal, Post Toasties, Corn Flakes"—and very few verbs, or as he puts it, "Those words . . . the ones that do things, that go places."

Playful naming is a rich source of humor in *Abel's Daughter*, as it is in Maddux's short stories. When Molly and Ted Demerest request a desk for their apartment, the landlord's description of it becomes its name: Nothing Elaborate; and a dresser is similarly named Halfway Decent. The family in the adjacent apartment, with whom the Demerests share a bathroom, have children named Gary Cooper, Rita Hayworth, and Joan Crawford. Not only is the family of the movie-star children not especially fastidious about the shared bathroom; they also have a penchant for cheap towels that quickly wear out, until finally "the complete center disappeared altogether and it hung, a limp picture frame, looped over the rack, like something in a Dali painting."

While references such as this one to Salvador Dali mark Molly Demerest's intellectual and experiential distance from the inhabitants of Chinkapink, she and Ted are immediately sensitive to the subtly nuanced hierarchies of the town. Most overt is the racial hierarchy that extends even to the black servicemen stationed nearby (they, too, must move to the back of the public bus). Among the white residents are great disparities in socio-economic levels, from the wealthy Lee Carter Higgins to the impoverished Mrs. Emerson. These differences are also related to race: Higgins is a committed racist who is bent on restoring to its former glory the ironically named Bewelcome, which had been a slave-breeding plantation before the Civil War, whereas Mrs. Emerson's poverty is in large part the result of her kindness toward blacks. Abel Loftis establishes a private hierarchy among the customers in his store through his practice of giving gifts to customers when they pay their bills: those he holds in high regard, such as Molly Demerest, get cans of expensive fruit cocktail, but a woman who condescends to Abel gets kidney beans.

Just as the memory of living in Occoquan remained vivid for Rachel Maddux, so the friendship between Molly and Serena endures past the Demerests' brief stay in Chinkapink in the form of a correspondence, and letters from Serena to Molly conclude the novel. After a decade of writing to Molly abut her family, her garden, and events in Chinkapink, Serena returns to the subject of race in her last letter, dated in June of 1954, shortly after the Supreme Court school desegregation decision. Far from being ecstatic, Serena is realistic about the actual effect the decision will have on the lives of black people in Chinkapink: "next September everything will be just the same that's what everybody knows, no matter what the Supreme Court say."

Abel's Daughter marks a shift in Rachel Maddux's book-length work from the large, ambitious canvas of *The Green Kingdom* to a more personal, often autobiographical writing that addresses social issues of deep concern to her. The culmination of this work was to be the nonfiction book *The Orchard Children*, an eloquent plea for a court system more attentive to the needs of children. And yet all of Maddux's work is distinguished by common elements: a passionate curiosity about the essences of human experience, a sense of wonder about the natural world, and a celebration of friendship and love.

Nancy A. Walker
Vanderbilt University

To my friend
Serena

1

IN CHINKAPINK there were two grocery stores. One was owned by white people and was called the Roebuck Grocery; the other was owned by Abel Loftis and was called the colored store. Abel Loftis was always in his store, and though, as I stepped out of the bright afternoon sunlight into the cool darkness of the store, I could only make out his huge shadow, I recognized his voice as he said to me, "Good evenin, Mrs. Demerest." Any time after noon, we had learned, was "evening."

"Good evening, Mr. Loftis," I said. As I moved toward the back of the store where the counter was I could see that he had someone with him.

"I like you to meet my daughter," he said. "Serena. She gone help me out while my son in the Army."

"Oh, are you Joey's mother?" I said.

And then it hit me, that face. What people ought to get back from their mirrors, and don't, that's what Serena's face gave out. I don't know how to describe the jolt of it, except that it was like meeting the real thing anywhere—the straight goods. It was

7

sobering, as though all the rest of the faces in the world were cari-
catures—overactive, exaggerated, grimacing. Not that you'd say
it was a beautiful face, though in time I came to think it so.

"Yes," she said, "Joey enjoying the books very much. I'll see
that he careful of them."

"If I ever get unpacked, I'll have some more for him," I said.

Another white woman came in the store then and Mr. Loftis
greeted her and then he turned to me. "And what can I get for
you today, Mrs. Demerest?" he said. And so I turned away from
Serena's face and got on with my grocery order. Mr. Loftis said
he'd send Joey down with the kerosene when he got home from
school.

When Joey came, he stuck his head around the door and I
wish I could paint that moment. Beneath the rich brown of his
face he held a bouquet of giant dahlias—red, gold, yellow and
orange. "These from my mother," he said. "You want me to put
the kerosene in the stove?"

"No, thanks, Joey. Since you taught me how to operate the
stove I can do it myself now."

"Yes, ma'am," he said.

"I met your mother today," I said.

"Yes, ma'am."

"You look like her, I think. Especially your eyes."

"Yes, ma'am," he said. "Everybody say I favor her."

The dahlias made a spot of life in that dreary place, so when
Ted got home from Fort Lassiter that night I had at·least this
much to offer. We sat on the miserable couch while we drank
our coffee and I told him about Serena and the dahlias. Gradually
I could feel myself getting wedged into the broken spring. The
overpowering effect of the room settled on us. Besides the sofa,
there were two old rocking chairs which took all the rest of the
floor space and one of those giant tables that are in Chinese restaurants.

"It's real grim, isn't it?" Ted said.

"Oh, well . . ."

8

"Disenchanted?"

"No," I said, "not really. It'll be better when . . ."

"Let's go to the woods," he said. "Let's say the hell with it."

Of course, the woods, the wonderful woods. That's why we were here. We had said if only we could live near those woods we would live in a tent, in the barest room, in anything. Out the back door, down the alley, three minutes' walk, and we were at the edge of the woods, as simple as that. Never had either of us lived where this was possible. To go to the woods had always meant planning and packing a lunch, arranging transportation and remembering to leave a note for the dry cleaner or the milkman, or somebody. In the months that followed, I never got over the thrill of flicking soap off my hands if the dishes were boring, walking to the woods, having time to discover a new plant and return, refreshed, before the dishwater was cold.

Already the path was familiar to us, as though it had been etched in our memories since childhood. Moss and oak leaves caressed our feet and, on both sides of the path, clinging to bushes and trees, the wild honeysuckle walled us in. We had the feeling not so much that noises were falling away with the light, but that, with the increasing darkness, silence was growing to a crescendo. At last we came to a place so quiet that our ears sang and here we paused for a moment, the more to appreciate what was coming. Within a few steps there was with us that sense of another presence which gradually became recognizable as sound, and then as the sound of water. As we walked on, the sound grew and grew until suddenly a roar coincided with a clearing in the path and there beneath us, swirling and crashing over rocks and boulders, was Chinkapink Creek.

We slid down the steep bank and carefully picked our way over the slippery stones to a big boulder where we sat with the water swirling all about us, wrapping us in a fine, cool mist. The violence of the noise absorbed us and after a time of readjustment we found our way to a place of absorption in it. We had the illusion of being afloat and hypnotized. The sound made talk

9

impossible. Perhaps this was why Ted liked this particular place. What was he thinking, I wondered. Was he, too, as I was, still wondering at the incredibility of our being here? By the most curious set of circumstances we had what everyone wants in wartime—the temporary interlude in an unwarlike place. How temporary, we didn't know. We hoped for three or four months. It was August, 1942.

Surrounded by the fine, cool spray of water, I could hardly believe that only a week before we had been sweltering in a hot hall bedroom in Lawtonville for which we paid ninety dollars a month. (As the landlady said, her family had been waiting since the War Between the States for the chance to make a nickel and she didn't intend to miss it now; we could take it or leave it.)

Ted had spotted Chinkapink from the air on a routine flight and, though we should have been hunting a cheaper place to live, we had decided on that fateful Sunday to get out of the city and go exploring instead. "It can't be far," he had said, "and it's sure to be cool near the creek." The bus driver had never heard of Chinkapink so we rode as far as Hester with him and decided to ask directions there. According to our map, it couldn't be more than three miles from Hester to Chinkapink and we felt sure there would be a local bus between the two towns.

But there wasn't.

"How do the people in Chinkapink get out?" we asked the man in the filling station at Hester.

"Them people in Chinkapink," he said, "if they don't have cars, they don't *come* out. That town's been dying for fifty years. No highway, no railroad, no nothing. Someday the vines gonna grow over that road and that'll be it."

We decided to walk. The vines had not grown over the narrow road yet, but weeds and bushes grew high on both sides of it. The road was paved, but in very poor repair. It was curving and quiet, all downhill, and not a car on it. After a couple of miles the sides of the road became clear of wild growth and we saw a few houses. The road turned abruptly and, under our feet, we discovered old, worn bricks rounded by time and stained green with moss. We were on the main street of Chinkapink and the sound of our own footsteps echoed indecently.

"But where is everybody?" I said, and realized I was almost whispering.

"Well, it's Sunday, after all," Ted said. "Maybe they're all in church."

"Maybe they're all dead."

Very hot from our long walk, we longed for a cool drink but there seemed to be no place to get one. We walked past a lumberyard, the post office, a grocery store, a bank, all closed. Across the street we could see a lunchroom sign on a small house, but it also was closed. Next to the lunchroom was a two-story brick building with a mock Georgian front.

"How did *that* get here?" Ted said. The building, so new, so neat, with its freshly painted white pillars, was incongruous on this street of one-storied frame buildings showing age, disrepair and neglect. The new building had no sign on it. In any other place it would have been an apartment house.

Further down on our side of the street there was a drugstore and, across from it, a movie in what appeared to be a barn. Both were closed. Now we were at the end of the street and here was the bridge Ted had seen from the air and beside it an old mill, deserted. Now we could see high above us the huge, chewed-out side of a cliff showing raw red clay. It dwarfed the whole town. And suddenly, at the end of the street, there was the path beckoning into deep woods.

"Let's take it," Ted said. "It'll be cool in there and we can rest and maybe later the lunchroom or the drugstore will be open."

That day (it seemed years ago) we had found our way to this very boulder where now we sat, having walked out of the "grim" room, leaving behind Serena's brilliant dahlias. We had taken off our shoes and stockings and put our tired feet into the cold, frothy water. The heat and our tiredness, even our thirst, went away, and the longer we stayed the more dreadful life in a city bedroom seemed. When we had at last left the boulder for the path where we could hear each other, I had said, "I never wanted to live any place so much. It breaks my heart."

"I know," Ted said. "I've been sitting down there trying to tell myself it would be worth walking twelve miles to the Fort every morning that I missed one of those buses at Hester."

"Anyhow," I said, "if the lunchroom's open, or the drugstore, let's ask around just for fun. Maybe in that new brick building we could get put on a list and it would be something to think about, at least. Didn't it look like an apartment house to you?"

"I thought business offices at first," Ted said. "But there weren't any signs on the building. What else could it be but apartments?"

We dreaded to go back into Chinkapink because we hated to hear for sure that there was no place to live and no practical way to the Fort, but at last we did put our shoes and stockings on and started down the path. If we had stayed any longer, we would have started planning how we could get a tent and live in the woods.

The drugstore was open this time and, though the owner had neither any knowledge of places for rent nor food to eat, he said we should ask of Taylor Frye for both. A very fat man stood in front of the movie and we crossed the street to ask him if he knew any places for rent and he, too, said if there were any, Taylor Frye in the lunchroom would know. When we passed the red brick apartment building we decided to go in and see if we could speak to the manager. There were several doors off the central hall but none said "manager." There were no doorbells, either. One of two large double doors was slightly ajar and Ted looked in.

"All I can see is rows of seats," he said. "Looks like a church or an auditorium. Nobody's there."

12

"Open the door further," I said. "Maybe the minister is still there."

We stepped inside where we could see the whole room and stepped right out again, hurried down the hall and out the front door and stood on the street paralyzed in helpless laughter from the shock of it. There had been one person in the room all right, lying very dead in his casket, with flowers all about him, everything ready and waiting for his funeral. I waited until we were decently away from the building. "What else could it be but apartments?" I mocked Ted.

"Still want to get on their waiting list?" he said.

We agreed that, before we blundered into something else, we had better go to the lunchroom and ask for Taylor Frye, as we had been told. "We should have known, really," Ted said. "In a dying town, there would logically be only one business profitable enough to support a new building."

Just then a middle-aged man came out of the lunchroom and sat on a porch chair. He was an extraordinary sight, particularly here. It was not only his expensive clothes, of the kind advertised as "California casual," or the air of having the world by the tail, which his manner of sitting and his calm lighting of a cigar seemed to demonstrate; it was that everything about him shouted *health*. On this street of muted, faded tones his bright red cheeks, his shining, carefully groomed gray hair, his look of having been scrubbed, and the big diamond on his cigar-wafting hand—all were dazzling. Another man, entering the lunchroom, greeted him: "How are you, Mr. Frye?" The dazzling creature smiled and slapped one plump thigh. "Very few people feel better than I do this morning," he said. "Very few people."

"Oh, are you Mr. Taylor Frye?" Ted said.

From the throne of his magnificent health, he looked upon us with patience. "I am *Mister* Frye," he said. "Taylor is my boy. Did you wish to see him?"

"Yes, we do."

"He'll be over pretty soon," he said. "You go on in the lunch-room and wait. I'll send him in."

While we waited for Taylor we had lunch. The extraordinary individuality of the faces of the other diners compared with the faces in a city lunchroom crowd heightened our sense of impending disappointment that we would not be able to live here. When Taylor came, we understood at a glance why he would be a boy all his life. Even if his magnificent father should ever die, Taylor would never think of himself as a Mister. Not in this life would he ever be able to lose his look of anxiety, of being behind in the long list of errands upon which he had been sent.

"But I had just what you want," he said, "and I rented it only last night." He managed to give us the feeling that if only he could undo the last twenty-four hours he could change not only the course of our lives but the course of his own. "There's nothing else for rent," he went on. "This lieutenant came here and gave me a deposit. It isn't only that I gave him my word," he said, as though people were constantly demanding of him that he go back on his word, "it's that it's for his *bride*."

Well, there we were. Who is so mean as to wish ill fortune to a bride? We could envy her, though. "Imagine," I said to Ted after we had paid our check and gone outside for a last look at the town. "Just imagine. For newlyweds to get a break like this in wartime—a quiet, leisurely place, with privacy, where everybody wishes you well."

Ted stopped and turned back to the lunchroom. "I just found a card in my pocket," he said, "with our telephone number on it." He scribbled his name on the card. "I'll leave it with Taylor Frye, in case the lieutenant breaks his neck or something."

Two days later I had a call from Taylor Frye. "You still want the place?" he said. Cold shivers ran up and down my spine. We hadn't meant it, really. Really, not his *neck*.

"What happened to the lieutenant?" I asked fearfully. "Or . . . or his bride?"

"Oh," Taylor said, "he brought her out to see the place and

she put on a regular fit. Said she was used to going out every night. Said there was nothing to do here, that she'd lose her mind in a place like this."

"O.K.," I said. "How soon can we come?"

"I'll be down next Sunday," he said. "I'll help you move your stuff."

Taylor Frye moved us into the house in Chinkapink in his hearse. "Hope you don't mind," he said. "I couldn't get your things in the ambulance, the pickup's full of fishing gear and my father's using the car."

The sight of the house marred the enchantment a little. There were three small square boxes set in a row for living room, bedroom and kitchen, and we were to share the bath with the people who lived on the other side of the hall. The contents of the first box I have already mentioned. In the second room there was an old iron bed, period. In the third there were a kitchen table, two chairs, a coal-oil stove which I didn't know how to operate, and an icebox. There were no curtains at any of the windows and the bathroom was filthy.

"Got to get the hearse back for a funeral now," Taylor said. "I'll come back this evening and take you down to Abel Loftis' grocery store. That is, if you don't mind trading with a colored man . . ."

"We don't," we said.

"Well, he's honest, and everybody trades there and I'm sure you'll be able to find someone who'll give you a ride to the Fort."

"Oh, fine," Ted said. "That twelve-mile walk has me worried."

"There's sure to be someone," Taylor said. "Lots of folks down here work at the Fort."

We had missed seeing the Abel Loftis Grocery before because it was on a side street. There were no street lights in Chinkapink and in the rosy evening dusk the light from the store made a solid yellow shaft. As we learned later, the store was the social center of the colored section and, as we crossed the threshold that first night with Taylor Frye, it didn't seem possible that this one room could hold so many people. They stood in groups of two or three, talking and drinking Cokes. As we entered, the talking dwindled to a ragged stop, leaving deserted and alone somebody's few notes of laughter. At the far end of the room was a large colored man bent over the counter, speaking to a tow-headed white child.

"David, Little David, play on your harp," he said. "And what does your mamma want?"

"Loaf of bread," David said.

The man straightened up then and we could see the size of him. "Evenin, Mr. Frye," he said. "What can I do for you?"

We advanced through the store, a path having silently been made for us. "Abel," Taylor Frye said, "these are my new tenants, Lieutenant and Mrs. Demerest."

"Good evenin, Mrs. Demerest," he said.

"Good evening, Mr. Loftis," I said.

"And good evenin, Captain," he said to Ted.

"Good evening, Mr. Loftis," Ted said.

There was a split second of immobility as though the store had just experienced a tremor. Even Little David (play on your harp) had one arm uplifted, waiting for his loaf of bread. Then Mr. Loftis smiled, reached for a pad of sales tickets, and put them down on the counter. "You like to have a charge account, Captain Demerest?" he said.

It was our turn to exhale, for we had somehow to live through a whole month on a week's pay, and now it had all been solved. First, Little David had to be taken care of, and then the credit system was explained to me and I have never seen a better one. In your own hand you wrote down your own order and when you were through you put your own pad back in its own pigeon-hole in a rack. If, at the end of the month, you questioned any purchase, you would be questioning your own record of it.

Taylor took Ted off to find a ride to the Fort for the next morning while I was laying in that same set of supplies that must be bought over and over again for each new town and for which one never keeps the list. Ted came back alone, Taylor Frye having as always some urgent errand calling him, and announced that he had a ride to Fort Lassiter arranged.

When I thought I had finished shopping, Mr. Loftis gently reminded me that without fuel I could not cook anything I had bought. It did not surprise him that I had no container and he reached in his pocket and pulled out a small flat piece of wool. This he unfolded into a fez, clapped it on his head, disappeared out the side door, and returned with a can full of coal oil. For such a large man he moved very rapidly and lightly, and he had replaced the fez in his pocket and stopped the spout of the can with a potato in the time it took Ted to hoist the big box of groceries onto his shoulder. He escorted us to the door. "We generally open till midnight ever night," he said. "Any time you want anything, I'll be here. Just any time."

It had turned night while we had been in the store and now it took all our attention to keep our footing on the rounded, settling old bricks. Someday our feet would know them by heart. It was still new to us, and the sound that our own feet made bounced back at us like pellets thrown from the hills. Sitting in a bowl, as the town did, made it a perfect echo chamber.

"A charge account at the grocery store and a ride to work arranged," I said. "We've nothing to worry about except how to operate that kerosene stove."

"This guy I'm going to ride with," Ted said, "he's a colored man with blue eyes and red hair. Name's Clarence Rochelle. It's real startling."

"I guess I hadn't really thought much about being in the South," I said. "Lawtonville was so full of Army it didn't hit me as southern the way Chinkapink does. I wonder why Taylor took us to the colored grocery?"

"I'm pretty sure it isn't why you hope it is," Ted said, "be-

17

cause on the way over to Rochelle's, Taylor gave me a little lecture to set me straight."

"Oh?"

"He just wanted to explain to me that 'down here we don't call them mister.' "

"What did you say?"

"Oh, I said it seemed a real friendly place, that we'd noticed how many people called him by his first name."

"Did he get sore?"

"No, he just thinks I'm stupid. I think, in a town this size, we're probably pawns in a feud between Taylor and the white grocery store."

"It'll be a pleasure to be a willing pawn for once."

"It'll probably turn out the white store wouldn't give him wholesale prices for his lunchroom, or something like that," Ted said.

In the darkness we stumbled up our own front steps and took the shock of the bare, ugly rooms when the lights were turned on, and then we tackled the kerosene stove.

Next day Taylor Frye dropped by to explain to me that he just wanted to be sure that we understood that *down here* things were probably a lot different from what we were used to and that *down here* we didn't call Abel Loftis mister. Everybody called him Abel.

"Will everybody call me Molly?" I said. "I'd like that."

He gave an exasperated sigh and turned to go, but then his eye was caught by a man we could see through the back window. Directly behind our yard was the rear of the white grocery store and a man now carried a crate of something out the back door and loaded it into the grocery truck.

"Now there," Taylor said, "see that fellow? He drives the grocery truck. You being new here and all, you wouldn't know unless someone took the time to tell you. He's colored."

"His skin's white," I said.

18

"Yes it is," Taylor said. "That's why I wanted to tell you because you might easily be mistaken."

"I might," I said, "easily. His hair's brown, too."

"He's got gray eyes, too," Taylor said, "but everybody here calls him John Quincy."

"Why?" I said.

"That's his name," he said. "His first two names, that is."

"What's his last name?"

"Now, Mrs. Demerest, that's what I'm talking about. You don't say his last name because he's colored."

"How can you tell?"

"Well, somebody tells you, like I'm explaining to you now."

"But if his skin's white and his hair's brown and his eyes are gray," I said, "that's the way I tell if somebody's white."

"I know," he said, "you might get mixed up, so that's why I stopped by to explain it to you."

"But how do *you* know he's colored?" I said.

"Why everybody around here knew his grandma, that's how."

"My grandmother's dead," I said. "What do I do?"

"Now, Mrs. Demerest," he said, "you know perfectly well what I mean."

"One thing interests me," I said. "Your speech doesn't sound southern to me."

"Of course not," he said. "You think I came from here? Why, if I came from here I'd be broke, tired, mortgaged to the bank for the clothes on my back. It takes somebody from outside to come into a place like this and take over their failures and make something out of them. *We* came from Ohio."

"Why are you working so hard on me, then?"

"You can believe me or not, Mrs. Demerest, but I'm trying to save you trouble. People like us, from Up North, we think we know how it is. But we don't. It's different. It's a lot different from what you think."

All these puzzling things I turned over in my mind while Ted and I sat on the big rock, lost in the roar of the water.

These were the woods we had wanted. They hadn't seemed southern woods, or woods *down here,* but just woods. Two weeks ago, to find a place to live near these woods had seemed our biggest problem. The sun dropped behind the huge red bluff and suddenly I shivered. Ted and I made signs to each other to go and, stepping carefully over the slippery rocks, we regained the shore, climbed the bank and started for home.

"What were you thinking on the rock?" Ted said. "You looked worried."

"Oh, about all of them here—Taylor Frye and Mr. Loftis and Serena, and how when you saw it from the air, this place, it looked so sheltered, so peaceful."

"Yes," he said. "I have the feeling every time I talk to Taylor Frye that I've enlisted in the wrong war."

"He was at me again today about it," I said. "But somehow I can't seem to stay mad at him."

"Well, no, when you ignore his talk and just pay attention to his acts."

"Like the rent," I said. "It's fair."

"Yes, and after all he did take us to Mr. Loftis. No matter his motive, it's different from trying to keep customers away from him."

"And he's afraid," I said.

"Taylor? What makes you think so?"

"Oh, not for himself. It's for us, somehow. I feel it."

Home once again, the vase of dahlias stabbed at the dreariness and reminded us of Serena. "The little boy, Joey," Ted said. "What's his last name and where's his father?"

"His name's Covington," I said. "Serena is a widow. Joey told me."

2

I NEEDED A DESK worse than anything. On the way into the living room, to plan where I would put it if I got it, I tripped over the rockers of one of the chairs. Both of us did every time we went through the room. For some reason we could not accustom ourselves to make allowance for them, and this time, as I once again saved myself from falling, it dawned on me that the rockers could perhaps be taken off the two chairs and that this would add some ten square feet of space to the room. Well, there it was done, once again. In all the places where we were to live there was always that time of camping like strangers and then, in each place, there would be the time of the first act of changing things, and after that, one could see how it would be, and the plan would take shape.

While I was examining the chairs to see how difficult it would be to remove the rockers (it turned out to be no trouble at all; only a light tap with a hammer and they fell off) I heard a rattling in the kitchen that meant, once again, we had a place with mice. I knew by now that it was futile to become excited. The only thing to do was to buy a trap and set it. Now there was a knock at the door.

It was the elusive Mrs. Wilkie from across the hall. I had seen glimpses of her on my way to the bath. She had always been halfway in or out of her door and I had never seen all of her at once. Apparently I would not this time, either, for she had been interrupted with only one of her eyebrows painted on, and this one, the right one, like an exaggerated circumflex accent, made the round blue eye beneath it seem to shout, "ô as in orb, lord." Her left arm she held protectively over her chest, as though she had been wounded. And if this were not startling enough, she said to me with desperation: "Is Gayee Coopah in your place? He's hidin from me."

It suddenly occurred to me that this might be, not madness, but motherhood speaking, for I had heard the patter of small feet, sometimes a sharp yelp, and a little quickly hushed crying, and someone with a remarkably poor aim shared the bathroom. "Come in," I said. "Is Gary Cooper your little boy?"

Mrs. Wilkie, still carefully protecting her chest, stepped in the room timidly. "He's teasin me," she said. "He took one of my—you know—" here she jogged the protective elbow, "ah call them mah powdah puffs, and he ran off with it and he's hidin someplace. Ah looked all ovah."

I remembered the mouse. Might it not be Gary Cooper hiding among the pots and pans? "Maybe he's in the kitchen," I said. "I heard a noise in there."

Sure enough, when I opened the lowest cupboard door, a tell-tale shoe showed. Mrs. Wilkie knelt down on the floor, still carefully protecting her flat chest. "Gayee Coopah," she said, "you come outa theah."

For answer, the shoe now disappeared from sight and a couple of pot lids clattered into a skillet. Since we had no closets, nor drawer space, our clothing was also in these cupboards and I had a sudden picture of Gary Cooper with his elbow in my one good hat. Mrs. Wilkie sat back on her heels and pointed the circum-

22

flex eyebrow at me, hopelessly. "He knows ah caint go out without it, the little devil," she said. "Ahm so flat chested, ah wouldn't be seen on the street." She stuck her head inside the cupboard again. "Gayee Coopah," she said, "if you don't bring me mah powdah puff, I won't go get you no cookies." Now she sat on her heels again and explained to me: "He won't eat nothin but cookies, juss one kind. Ah don't know what to do. If ah don't get him cookies, he don't eat nothin at all. He hasn't eat nothin but cookies for two months."

"You have a little baby, too, don't you?" I said, for I had seen a bootie on the hall floor, lying flat and discarded, and much too small for Gary Cooper.

"Yes," she said. "Rita Haywuth. And then there's a girl, too, youngah than Gayee Coopah."

"What's her name?"

"Joan Crawfud," she said.

Gary Cooper suddenly slithered out of the cupboard, evaded his mother's lunge and was off into the hall. Mrs. Wilkie, angry now, forgot her wounded chest and ran after him. But I felt sure that she would not find the lost article on him. I crawled into the cupboard and found the false breast neatly and logically fitted inside a sugar bowl on which the lid had been carefully replaced. He had a good sense of form, that boy. I lay half in the tight cupboard, trapped by helpless laughter and the relief of finding my good hat intact.

I delivered the "powder puff" next door. Joan Crawford and Rita Hayworth stared silently out of their pale blue eyes. Somewhere in the distance Gary Cooper cried in a halfhearted whine. Later I saw them all leave, Joan Crawford holding on to her mother's hand, Rita Hayworth in Mrs. Wilkie's arm, and Gary Cooper trailing behind. They were going to walk one block to the main street and there enter the Roebuck Grocery to purchase the necessary cookies, no doubt. For this event, during which perhaps five or six people might see her, Mrs. Wilkie must armor herself with three-inch heels and both "powder puffs" firmly

23

anchored. Her face was now complete with a Katharine Hepburn mouth and another circumflex eyebrow. There were small curls in contour planting all over her head. She wore a flowered summer dress which had a ruffle around the hem and, as they passed even with the window, I saw the extraordinary thinness of the arm which held Rita Hayworth.

This terrible thinness seemed to be the Wilkies' mark in everything. Even their one towel which hung in the bathroom so testified. Little larger than a face towel, it hung on a rack facing me each day as I bathed. Slowly the center of it became transparent so that I could make out the wall behind it. As its substance began to disappear, its odor increased.

The day we moved in, Taylor Frye sent the colored man who worked for him, Jim Lawrence, over to clean the bathroom. He was the most handsome man, white or colored, in all Chinkapink. He was very tall and slender and his skin was the color of copper. He was very fastidious about his clothes and on Sunday nights sat in Mr. Loftis' Grocery, drinking Coke, dressed with a quiet and expensive elegance. All other times he and Taylor Frye were inseparable. He was so dreadfully out of place in that filthy bathroom that I could not bear to watch him, but he said nothing and worked long and quietly, and when he was through every inch of the room sparkled. After that I scrubbed the bathroom with soap every day, as I would have anyhow had it been all ours, but the dampness absorbed increasingly more odor from the dwindling Wilkie towel. I grew to hate this towel, as though it were human. Finally, the complete center disappeared altogether and it hung, a limp picture frame, looped over the rack, like something in a Dali painting. At last it disappeared, to be replaced by another just like it which also began to be transparent in the center.

My knowledge of childhood poverty which I carried with me from Kansas was a far different thing from this thinness of the Wilkies. When I remembered the sound of children crying, its characteristic was a bellow of rage instead of a whine. We were

24

more likely to get a black eye or a broken nose than decayed teeth, and children bore the names of their grandmothers rather than those of movie stars. The monotony of homemade vegetable soup eaten at someone else's direction is not the same as the monotony of cookies eaten at one's own. No matter how authoritarian, violent, even brutal the direction might have been, it wasn't in the hands of children.

Must every relevant magazine or newspaper article I had read be re-examined now? Must I remember that a high percentage of individuals in a lynching mob might be named for movie stars and hands that plant fiery crosses might be sticky with marshmallows?

It seemed an excellent time to go for a walk, what with all the things I had to mull over, and here again I faced a sudden disorientation, for I found that I could not confidently read the weather, either. There was a strange light over everything that might mean rain or snow or violent wind. I decided on a raincoat and headed in the direction opposite from the creek where I usually went. The day before, I had come upon an old green bottle of an interesting shape and somewhere on the road to Hester I had seen a bright red vine that would be wonderful in it. Shortly after I started out, the air became filled with mist. There was no real rain, so that I did not actually feel wet, just this astringent and palpable atmosphere clothing me in isolation. So fine was the mist that I was able to light a cigarette and keep it going without trouble. I left the road and struck off in the direction of a sparse woods, conscious of an extraordinary sense of well-being. The mist played strange tricks with the visibility. Nearness and distance kept exchanging places, as though I had stumbled on dreamstuff.

I began to hum and I put my hands in my pockets. There I found a few old peanuts in the shell. Remembering the day, months ago, when we had been to the zoo, it seemed to me that I remembered two strangers. They seemed terribly innocent, that they had not that day at the zoo had even an inkling that they would be now in this so different a place.

I picked some oak leaves that were mottled with gold and orange and, to add to the misty, enchanted quality of the atmosphere, the branches snapped off effortlessly in my hands. Further on I saw a single strand of a scarlet runner climbing up a tree, its leaves like red stars against the trunk, and I hurried on to it and reached up my hand.

"That's right," I heard, as though the tree itself had spoken. I whirled about and there, not a foot away, was a creature so still, so camouflaged, that I might easily have walked into her. "If you see anything you want, just take it," she said.

Under my raincoat I could feel goose pimples rising on my arms. It gave me an eerie feeling to think that piece of solidified mist might have been watching, motionless, as I cracked the shells of the stale peanuts and tossed them into my mouth, as I had walked along humming and breaking off the oak branches.

"And if you see anything in the yard you want, just come in and get it, too," she said.

But there was no "yard" that I could see; we were surrounded by wild growth. I moved a step nearer the creature, but my questions died in me. She was a white woman, incredibly old. She had no teeth and her pointed chin was covered with long white hairs. Her eyes were like those of a blind setter—rheumy, brown-lidded, the irises a pale, filmed blue. Her skin was brown and mottled, and over her head she had tied an old woolen rag. It kept slipping over her forehead. An ancient brown coat from which the collar had been removed was fastened at her neck by a giant safety pin. Under the coat, a nightgown hung down, its hem resting tiredly on the wet weeds. Her feet were completely covered by the gown. Her tiny brown hands had been twisted into bird claws by rheumatism and these she held against her body.

Whether the mist had actually thinned or my eyes had been sharpened by the fright, I now saw, at some distance behind the creature, the faint mark of a path leading to a solid, brooding structure that must be a house. It was large and square, all its windows covered by heavy wooden shutters. The paint was completely gone from it, leaving the boards the soft, lavender color of age, so that if it had not been for its squareness, it, too, could easily have been part of the mist. It seemed to have lost all memory of ever having held life.

"Oh," I said, "is that your house? Excuse me, I had no idea there was a house here. I thought this was a woods."

"Yes," she said, and it was still as though words were coming from a tree or some other rooted thing, for she made no movement, showed no change of expression. "Mr. Emerson said (Mr. Emerson is my husband), he said, 'I want to build you a big house because you've got three children,' but I said, 'No, just build me a small house like Grandmother Daniels' up the road.' 'You're a damn fool,' he said to me. 'I want to build you a big house, a square house, because you've got three children.' 'The children'll be gone from us soon enough,' I said. 'They won't be bothering us long.' 'You talk like a damn fool,' he said to me. That's all he could ever think of to call me—a damn fool. He had to go into a naval hospital in Philadelphia and I never saw him again. He had a pension and sent me some of it. I was thankful for it."

"I'm sorry to have intruded on you," I said. "We've just moved to Chinkapink and . . ."

"No," she said, "I don't like to ask my neighbors for so much as a meal."

I told her my name, and suddenly her manner seemed to change. With one twisted claw she shoved the rag back from her forehead and turned that rooted body toward the huge, looming house behind her. A slit opened in her face and I realized that a smile was intended. "I love this house," she said. "I've lived here fifty years. Eleven rooms it has. I love the dear people I come in contact with."

27

And yet it seemed impossible that she ever came "in contact with" anything but squirrels, birds or cats.

"You live in Chinkapink?" she said, as though it were some fabulous, distant city.

"We're new," I began.

"Some people say the ladies of Chinkapink is just damn fools but I say they shouldn't talk like that." She bent her head down toward her chest, as though dismissing me, and the old rag slipped over her forehead. "You know how some people are," she said. "They get hold of an idea and they're reluctant to part with it."

Holding my branch of oak leaves (I couldn't bring myself to ask for the red vine), I began to back away. "Good-by, Mrs. Emerson," I said. But she had become once again a tree standing rooted and motionless, staring at nothing, an ancient tree upon which the mist gathered and ran in rivulets.

When I got home I changed into dry shoes, took off my raincoat, and brushed the peanut shells out of the raincoat pockets. Remembering the pleasure it had given me to find them there, I tore off one of the speckled oak leaves and tucked it in the pocket. Would we be in still another place by the time I wore the coat again, and would this day, this town, and old Mrs. Emerson seem far away?

Since the coffee supply was low I made a pot of cocoa, and while it was heating I put the oak leaves in the green glass jar and went through the bedroom to stand in the living-room doorway, for ever since this morning, when I had thought of taking the rockers off the chairs, the room had gradually been taking shape in the back of my mind. It was always so in each new place, if we had any length of time at all. There would be the days or weeks getting located, having a roof over our heads and no more, and then there would be that first act of changing something which started the whole intricate process of putting down roots, of making the shelter speak for us and look like us and, in time, even take on our smell.

I dragged out one of the unpacked cartons which we called the "roots" box and, sipping my cup of cocoa, began to unpack the box. There were two India prints that would, but only just, fit the windows. Sometimes these were bedspreads, sometimes tablecloths, and sometimes so out of keeping that they were left unpacked. But here, with the mother-of-pearl Chinese table, we were on our way to an Oriental décor. I got a pad of paper and began a diagram of the room. In the northeast corner would go the Chinese table for Ted's desk. We could remove the great claw feet, I hoped, or saw them off, to make it the right height. Why is it that though these tables are supposed to have some connection with people who are much shorter on the average than Americans, they always hit at the armpit level? Well, for this the student lamp, and on the wall the print of "La Grande Jatte." Then in the southeast corner my desk, which Taylor Frye had promised. "I'll get you something," he said. "Nothing elaborate, but a desk of some kind." And over my desk would go Vermeer's "The Cook." Then between us, in front of the window curtained in the India print, we could make a bookcase out of our best wooden packing box.

On the north wall, which contained the other window, would go the abominable couch and at the northwest corner we would need another lamp. From the roots box came a piece of fabric, a heavy red linen with a design of deer in white. This over a footlocker would have to be the coffee table. On the west (bedroom) wall we could put one of the chairs, minus rockers, and the typewriter table. The other chair (rockerless) could go against the south wall, which was mostly taken up by the entrance door.

So we needed to buy a lamp, then, and some big comfortable ashtrays (the ones from the last place had all broken) and we would be once again deep in the settling process. Already I could see it, with Ted's blue Edgeworth tobacco can on the Chinese table, coffee ready in the silver pot on the linen-covered footlocker, and atop the "bookcase," before the India-print curtains, a great bunch of Mrs. Covington's dahlias. It meant one trip to the city, for I had seen no lamps at the lumberyard or hardware store, and no ashtrays anywhere. I longed for the time when we could use the saucers for saucers again and bury in some deep place the one, small, stinking metal tray which we had found in the house and whose legend I read twenty times a day: STOLEN FROM THE 211 CLUB.

The roots box also produced the silver coffeepot (much tarnished), two silver candle holders, an antique butter dish, our art books, and several lengths of deep blue theatrical gauze. This time the blue gauze could be kitchen curtains, I decided.

Joey had a special knock which I recognized now, so I called to him to come in without having to disentangle myself from the contents of the roots box.

"This note stuck in your front door," he said.

"Oh?" I said. "Somebody must have been by while I was out in the woods." I opened the note, which was from Taylor Frye, and read: *Mrs. Demerest, Have desk for you (nothing elaborate). Can your husband come over for it when he gets home? Have to hold funeral.*

"I'm going to get a desk at last, Joey," I said.

"Yes, ma'am," he said. "What's in that book? I never saw a book that size."

"Paintings," I said. "Reproductions. Want to look at it?"

"Yes, ma'am."

"You carry it, Joey, and let's go out to the kitchen and have some cocoa while we look at it."

"Yes, ma'am," he said.

While I basted a top hem in the India prints for the rod to go through (always baste in the Army; the windows will be different in the next town), Joey sipped his cocoa and slowly turned the pages of the book. When he came to "The View of Arles" he was quiet for a long time. Finally he pointed to the background and said, "This part here must be way up in the air."

"It looks behind the front part to me," I said.

30

"Yes, ma'am," he said.

I tried to think how it might have looked to me when I was twelve. When is it one "accepts" perspective? Since I couldn't remember, it must have been very early. Did Joey, then, see no pictures? But where had I? My own childhood had certainly not been filled with trips to art galleries. There were illustrated books, of course, always, and there was school.

"Do you have many paintings in your school, Joey?"

"No, ma'am," he said. "None. There's a picture of Jesus hang in the church, but it not bright." Automatically he put up his arms in the position of crucifixion. "This very good cocoa," he said.

A school without a single painting in it—it seemed hard to believe. "You go to this school up on the road to Hester?"

"No, ma'am," Joey said. "That's a white school. Colored all go to Montrose."

"Montrose? Why, that's twenty-five miles from here. How do you get there?"

"Bus," he said. "Bus comes at six o'clock in the morning. Picks up all the colored in Montrose County. Takes till ten o'clock before we get to school."

"What time do you get home?"

"About dark. Orvil Johnson he drives the bus. He get so mad every day. The children always eatin their lunch on the way to school. And every day he say: 'Children, don't eat your lunch before you get to school. What you gone eat lunchtime?' "

"But Joey, the little ones in the first grade. Surely they aren't gone twelve hours a day."

"Yes, ma'am. It's all the same. I remember I always asleep when I got home. Sarah, my sister, she have to carry me."

"Where is Sarah?" I said. "I never see her around the store."

"No, ma'am. She always home studyin. She gone graduate from high school next year. She all the time make notebooks, notebooks. She make A's in school."

"And you're not quite such a scholar?"

"No, ma'am," he said. "Not me."

"Joey, you don't have to keep saying *yes ma'am, no ma'am,* to me all the time."

"Yes, ma'am," he said, automatically, and then he hit himself on the head. "That just happen before I think. What do I say, then?"

"Well, can't you call me Molly the way I call you Joey? You make me feel as though I were your teacher or your grandmother or something. I just want to be your friend."

"But wouldn't it seem funny someone my . . . my age callin somebody . . . your age by her first name?"

"I don't think so. But if you can't do it, I can call you *sir.* Just so we can talk together."

"Yes, ma'am," he said, and bit his lip and hit himself on the skull.

We both laughed and I poured some more cocoa for us. Joey went back to the book of paintings. At the "Pietà" he stopped. I wondered if he would ask the meaning of the word or if, even, the figure would seem to him to be Christ at all. Finally he said, "I like the sky in this one."

"Look, Joey," I said, "you can have two of them for your own. Maybe your mother would like one, too. You can take the book home with you and then later bring it back and tell me which ones you'd like and I'll get Ted to take them out with a razor blade."

"Cut the book?" he said.

"Sure," I said. "That's what it's for. See that dotted line there? It's all right, only I could never get it straight myself. You take all the time you want to decide."

"Yes," he said. "There, did you hear that? I just said *yes* that time instead of *yes ma'am.*"

"Don't worry about it, Joey. Maybe it will come naturally after a while."

"But if I don't say yes ma'am to you . . ."

"Yes, Joey. What is it?"

32

"Well, I . . . I . . . I might forget and not say it to somebody I'm supposed to."

"Oh," I said. "Well, Joey, I didn't think of that. You see, I'm new here. I'm ignorant about the ways. Let's not worry about it. Let's forget it and see how it works out as time goes by. Would you like to practice on the typewriter?"

"Yes, ma'am," he said, and hit himself on the skull. "I . . . I . . . I just keep doing it," he said.

"There's some practice paper by the machine," I said. I knew children dearly loved to write on the typewriter and I hoped this might make him forget about yes ma'am and no ma'am for a while. I felt a fool for having made him so self-conscious that he had actually begun to stutter. While I finished the curtains, I could hear him pecking away patiently, overwriting the margin stop at each line and hunting for the release. After a while he came back to the kitchen, the Van Gogh tucked under his arm.

"I got to go now," he said. "I got to deliver afros for my cousin. He sick today."

"Afros?"

"*Afro-Americans*," he said. "It's a newspaper. Most all the colored take it. But I take the book home first, don't worry."

There were curtain rods at the bare windows, a rare thing in a rented house, and I was balanced precariously on a chair putting up the India prints when Ted came in. He lifted me down. "Roots again?" he said. "Don't you ever get discouraged?"

"Look," I said, showing him my diagram. "How'd you like this? If we took the rockers off the chairs and—oh, I almost forgot, Taylor Frye's got a desk if you can go over and get it."

"Sure," he said. "I'll go right away." He reached down to the mess of things around the carton, lifted an edge of the blue gauze in his fingers, touched the tarnished coffeepot, lifted and replaced one of the candle holders. His face had that look it gets when he sees as sad what I see as gallant.

"Maybe you'd better wait till after dinner. You don't want to move furniture on an empty stomach."

33

"You don't fool me with your solicitude," he said. "I know when the day comes you're ready to put down roots, you want the whole place made over by midnight. Just give me an apple or something."

"Now, listen," I said, as he started out the back door. "Just because you're ten feet tall, don't try to do it all by yourself. You can get a rupture just the same as anybody else. Get Jim Lawrence to help you."

"Haw," he said. "Caution. I never used a rocking chair for a ladder, anyhow."

But as it turned out, he didn't need Jim Lawrence. He carried the desk home on one hand, held high above his shoulder, it was that tiny. We just stood there laughing at the silly thing and then very formally Ted set the desk down and said, "Molly, I want you to meet Nothing Elaborate. N.E., this is Molly." And then he consulted my diagram as though it had been a complicated blueprint and, with great care, put Nothing Elaborate in the proper corner.

Well, there it was. You could imagine a very small girl seating herself at it to write, on "kiddy" stationery, *Dear Aunt Stella, thank you for the lace pincushion.* But what I had in mind was volume two of a novel which had already accumulated enough weight to crush the poor desk. Well, never mind. The novel I would write at the kitchen table, as I usually did anyhow, handy to the coffeepot. Nothing Elaborate at least had two drawers for stationery, and even I sometimes had to write letters beginning *Dear Aunt So-and-so, thank you for the . . .*

"Did you remember to borrow a hammer?" I said while we were having dinner.

"It's in the desk drawer," Ted said. "While I was over there, Taylor Frye's mother came out and wanted to know what you needed a desk for, so I told her you were a writer and Taylor said, 'That explains it, then. The postmaster told me she was getting mail under two names.' "

"Mr. Tibbs? And yet he never says anything to me except

yes indeed and *no indeed* and he has an absolute nothing expression."

"Tibbs?" Ted said. "Is that his name?"

"Not that I found out from him. *He's* not exchanging any confidences with an outsider. There's a thing on the wall, like an operator's license, that has the name of the postmaster filled in."

After dinner we took the rockers off the chairs and moved the couch. The Chinese table, minus claw feet, turned out to be just the right height. Already the room seemed twice as large and I couldn't wait until morning to put up "La Grande Jatte" and "The Cook" over the two desks. I turned on the student lamp and turned off the ghastly overhead light. Ted was staring at the four detached claw feet which he had lined up on Nothing Elaborate's top. "Seems as though we ought to be able to do *something* with them," he said.

He got out the big packing box, turned it on its side and made two shelves out of the top boards. "We don't have to unpack the books tonight, too, do we?" he said.

"No, I can wait till tomorrow. I just want to see how the oak leaves look, though, on top of the bookcase."

"Have you been to the woods today?" he said, and I realized I had not told him about Mrs. Emerson. Nor about Joey and "The View of Arles," nor about the *Afros*.

"Oh, and the *Afros*," I said. "Joey said he had to deliver the *Afro-American*. He said almost all the colored people here take it. And I just realized, I never saw a copy of any Negro newspaper, I don't think. How is it I never thought about this? I went to school with Negroes most of my life and yet it never occurred to me but what they were reading the same newspaper I was."

"Didn't you ever hear of the *Defender?* Or the *Call,* or the *Amsterdam News?*" Ted said. "They used to be for sale on the corner where we went to hear Pete Johnson and Joe Turner."

"I don't know how I missed them," I said. "I must have been

35

talking to the hot chitlins and crawdads man. But there must be many white people who never realize there is a Negro press. What I think is, though, if I did see a copy on a newsstand I'd think of it as a Negro paper. Does that mean that if Negroes see a newsstand where I go, they don't think Republican or Democrat, Liberal or Conservative or Reactionary, but just *white* paper?"

"You know it's after midnight?" Ted said.

As I began to pick up things and empty the saucers and STOLEN FROM 211 of cigarette butts, I came on Joey's practice paper.

Joey
Joey Covington
Dear Mrs. Demerest how are you? i am fine
Today is Thursday.
Roses are red
Vilets
Violets are blue
Joey Covington is crazy.
There was once another lady liked colored but the white people hate her. LOn ago. Long Ago.

I crumpled the paper and threw it into the waste basket, turned out the desk lamp and started to undress for bed. Ted, with his shirt half unbuttoned, was staring broodingly into the living room.

"Say," he said, "those things at the windows—weren't they bedspreads once, someplace?"

3

BY VIRTUE of having my shoulder jerked almost loose from its socket from trying to get into the locked door of the Chinka-pink Bank, I gradually learned the birthdays of Robert E. Lee and Jefferson Davis, the anniversaries of the Siege of Charleston, the Confederate victory at Bull Run, the First Confederate Congress, Confederate Memorial Day and the death of Robert E. Lee. The bank would be open, though, on Lincoln's birthday ("Why, ma'am, that's a *Yankee* holiday"). Anyhow, I did finally get that first paycheck deposited and so I was able to take up Taylor Frye's repeated offer to ride into Lawtonville. "Any time you want to shop," he had said, "I go to the city every other day and it generally takes me about two hours to get my errands done. No trouble at all to take you and bring you home." And so I got the ashtrays and a supply of candles and a lamp, the last few things we needed to be settled. One of Taylor's errands was "to pick you up something halfway decent for a chest of drawers." So at last Ted and I were to get our clothes disentangled from the pots and pans. It seemed to rain a little

37

every day now, so that the air was always damp and the clothes-line never empty.

Taylor's conversation was constantly filled with high drama, for his ambulance was called to wrecks on the highway at Hester and he had this need to relate the sight of blood and burning bodies and decapitations. But his concern that day was the death of Jasper Benoit, a colored man, husband to Lizzie Benoit, who tended Lou Ann Roebuck while her mother ran the white grocery store.

"Poor devil," Taylor said. "Fell off the roof and broke his back. Had a peg leg and should never have been on the roof, but the rains worried him and he wanted to get that roof shingled. He couldn't wait. Died instantly, though. *Right* now." (Later, when I looked for Jasper Benoit's death in the obituary column, I could not find it, and Ted pointed out to me that I was looking under DEATH NOTICES in large Old English type, instead of under COLORED DEATH NOTICE, printed in Gothic bold, in a separate column.)

"Does it always rain every day like this in the fall?" I said to Taylor.

"Not this early," Taylor said. "I never remember that it started so early like this. Things are beginning to be a mess. Mud everywhere."

At the bus station in Lawtonville, where Taylor Frye was to pick me up for the return journey, I went into the "white" toilet. I studied the wall writings, being amazed as I always am at the number of people who seem to have pencils handy when they need them. (Yet whenever I run into old friends on the street of a strange town and we wish to exchange addresses or phone numbers, no one ever seems to have anything to write with.) Among the customary and, apparently, universal comments on the walls was one I had never seen: I HATE ALL WHITE PEOPLE. PRETTY SOON THE JAPS WILL KILL ALL THE WHITE PEOPLE   HA HA   GOOD.

Was it not incredible that such feelings were confined to a

38

rare and harmless expression in writing and even more incredible that white people assumed it would be? How was it that white women confidently held their hands under a soap dispenser which had been polished by someone not allowed to use it, never anticipating that it might run sulphuric acid? How was it they bent smilingly to drink from a fountain that had been cleaned by someone who dared not quench his thirst there and never expected to have live steam spewed into their faces? And, most strangely of all, how was it they had, for generations, turned over to denied women the complete care of their children, knowing the children's throats would not be cut?

On the way home I mentioned to Taylor Frye that I had recently seen a book on the architecture of this region of the South and of how, in the mention of original owners of famous old houses, I recognized so many names that were to be heard in Chinkapink.

"Oh, yes," he said. "But now it's the trash man and the milkman and the ice man. You notice those fine boots Redley Stuart wears on the ice truck?" Redley Stuart had called on our first day to ask about bringing ice. He had come in the back door, followed by his hound, while a huge colored man waited in the truck. Stuart had drifted as though drawn to one of the kitchen chairs, his hound leaning tiredly against one of his legs. He wore elegant leather riding boots. He had sandy hair and the dry, thin skin that goes with it after youth is gone. His eyes were washed-out blue and there hung about him an air of fatigue, soft and unassuming, like his gentle, courteous voice.

"Redley never wears anything but those boots," Taylor went on, "but he hasn't been on a horse for twenty years. He's living in a slave cabin on his old place. Got just about enough land around it left to walk around the house. Someday he'll lose that, too. All the ones who had any gumption got out. Redley's got a brother sells cars in Lawtonville and a sister went Up North. But Redley, he's too tired to leave. That's the way it is with all those old families. The ones that stayed, they're all tired."

39

"He seems a very nice man," I said.

"Oh, Redley, he's a very nice man. But if anything ever happened to Benedict and Redley had to lift that ice off the truck himself, I hate to think."

I hated to think, too. It was almost impossible to imagine Redley Stuart without his silent, smiling giant, just as it was impossible to imagine Benedict without his hat. For if Redley Stuart had his boots, Benedict had a hat. It was a large-brimmed black hat, pinned up on one side like a pirate's hat, but in such a way that compartments were produced. Out of this hat Benedict could draw an ice pick, handkerchief, change purse, keys, scribbled memoranda, matches, cigarettes, and I never knew what else. I suppose it had originally been made of felt, but oil from his hands, sweat, rain and sun had produced the patina of fine black leather.

"Benedict's very patient with me," I said. "I never remember to empty the pan until I see him and that makes me think of it. By then it's so full it's too heavy to lift, so he generally lifts it for me."

After Taylor let me out at home, he went over to get Jim Lawrence to help him unload Halfway Decent, but before I put the clothes in the drawers I decided to go down to Mr. Loftis' store and pay the grocery bill. Mr. Loftis was waiting on two colored women when I went in the store and Joey was just finishing sweeping the floor. Mr. Loftis excused himself from his customers to go look over Joey's work. He took his time, as always. "Well, Joey," he said, "you did a good job. That look very nice. Very respectable."

"I suppose," one of the women said, "you hear about Jasper Benoit?"

"Such a tebble thing," the other woman said. "He almost finish with that roof. Maybe a few hours more and he be done. Him with that peg leg, he been workin and workin on that house all by hisself for weeks. You see Lizzie yet?"

"He fix up the banister and the porch. He had that little

house jus ready for winter. Lizzie she blame herself now she dint make him stop."

"The reason he died," Mr. Loftis said, "is they brag on him too much. It was good the way he had it, but people keep admirin, keep sayin how nice it look, and he kept wantin to make it better." He tidied the purchases together on the counter as a gentle reminder to the women to get on with their orders. He gave me a smile to show he knew I was waiting. "People should never brag on a one-legged man," he said. "It make him try too hard."

"Now, Mrs. Demerest," he said, when it was my turn. "What you like to have?"

"Oh, I just wanted to pay the bill," I said.

He reached into my pigeonhole and pulled out a stack of sales slips, all in my own handwriting, fastened together with a clip, an adding-machine tape on top with a check mark by each item. When I was ready to leave, he said, "You forgot your package."

"But I didn't buy anything," I said.

He held the brown paper sack out to me. "Well, we generally always give a little present when you pay your bill," he said.

It had been so at home when I was a child, but I had forgotten all about it and I had no idea there was any place left in the world where the custom continued. I was filled with delight and also confusion, for our custom had been that the children were given their choice of the candy, free (bacon strips, I chose, made of coconut), and now there was something heavy, a can, inside the sack, but I felt it would be indelicate to examine it.

As soon as I was safely outside, though, I looked. It was a large can of his most expensive brand of fruit cocktail. I did not know at the time but what this was the standard gift. Later, when I saw a loud-mouthed, ugly white woman who always ordered Mr. Loftis around ("Abel, you cut that meat right. Abel, don't give me no bad ones, heah?") get her gift of a can of kidney beans, I began to pay attention. In time, I learned Mr. Loftis' judgment of every charge customer he had, and Ted and I got so we could identify the people in the town as Old Kidney Bean, Sour Cherries, Horseshoe Plug, Red Pie Cherries (Pitted) and Miss Sauerkraut.

Mr. Loftis lived in a big two-storied house next door to the grocery store. It had a veranda all around it and sometimes Mrs. Loftis would appear there, standing and looking out, never smiling. She would nod to my greeting, but she never spoke. She never worked in the store. I don't know that she ever entered it. She was a very tall woman, very thin, with light colored skin, straight gray hair and large gray eyes. She was called Miss Addie, even by Joey. It seemed impossible that Miss Addie could be Serena's mother.

Joey came in soon after I got home. He was carrying a bouquet of dahlias in one hand and the Van Gogh book in the other. "My mother said tell you she sorry the flowers so beat from the rain," he said, "but she send them anyhow cause maybe they be the last."

"It was sweet of her to send them," I said. "You tell her thank you, will you?"

"Yes, ma'am," he said.

"Well, have you decided which pictures you want, Joey?"

"Yes, ma'am," he said, opening the book to a black-and-white reproduction. "My mamma she taken this colored one." Before I had time to express my confusion, he had flipped the pages over to "The View of Arles" and then to the "Pietà." "But I dint," he said. "I like the bright ones."

"Oh," I said, "I see. Well, Ted will take them out for us when he comes home."

"Can I use the typewriter?" he asked. "I have to write something fifty times cause I dint have my lesson today in egg."

"Egg?"

Egg turned out to be agriculture, of which two semesters were required, though, as Joey said, "No one ever gone have a farm; they all go work at the Fort."

"What do you want to do, Joey?" I said.

"I want to be a lectrician," he said.

He began his tedious typing while I put the flowers in water and started some cocoa. I could hear him sighing with terrible boredom and finally I came in and looked over his shoulder where he had written over and over:

$$100 = 4 \text{ weeks}$$
$$360 = 8 \text{ weeks}$$
$$800 = 12 \text{ weeks}$$
$$1300 = 16 \text{ weeks}$$

"One hundred what?" I said.

"Mash," Joey said, "for chickens. Hundred pounds feeds em for four weeks, and so on."

"Feeds how many chickens?"

"I don't know," he said, and he sighed. "It so silly anyhow. It's all written on the bag the feed comes in. We sell feed in the store sometimes. And it depend on what kind you buy."

Is this teacher bright? I wanted to ask, but I didn't mean bright or colored, I meant bright or stupid. "Listen, Joey, do you know this?"

"Yes, ma'am," he said, and recited it to me.

"All right," I said. "Go get yourself some cocoa and I'll type it for you. It's going to take you all night at this rate."

I could hear him pacing back and forth, back and forth, while I was typing and finally he came in, waited for me to stop typing and said, "Would you say your name for me once more?"

"Molly."

"I been practicin to say it," he said, "but I say it over so many times, it don't even sound like a name any more."

"Well, here's your chicken mash table fifty times, and you can bring me a cup of cocoa now."

When he handed me the cup he said, "Miss Molly, here's your cocoa," and then he looked shyly at me to see if this compromise would be accepted.

"Thank you, Joey," I said. Me, I just wanted out of the situation, and if this would put an end to his pacing the floor and pounding himself on the head I was grateful for it.

It began to rain again, as it seemed to every night now, and Ted was not home at dinnertime. It grew later and later and finally he stumbled in, soaking wet and limping.

"What *happened* to you?" I said, grabbing his raincoat off him.

He sank onto the couch and pulled off his soggy shoes. "God, I hate to tell you," he said. "It's such a pitiful, ridiculous little tale."

"Are you hurt? You're limping. Were you in an accident?"

"Oh, no," he said. "Nothing so dramatic. I've got a blister on one heel."

I got him some hot coffee and sat down on the floor to pull off his socks. "Have you had dinner?" I said, sucking in my breath at the sight of the inflamed heel.

"Oh, no," he said, "I haven't done anything sane like eat a meal. Today I just did idiot things." He laughed tiredly and shook his head. "Of all the futile gestures," he said.

"Bus?" I said, because this had happened to both of us now several times that a bus on which one or both of us were passengers would stop suddenly and the driver would ask a colored passenger to move back or a white passenger to move forward. Sometimes they would refuse politely, always in a northern accent, and we could feel how the other white passengers bristled, whether it was from a white man or colored, knowing if we too must protest, as generally we found we must, our accent would be taken so emotionally that no *word* we said, however calm or reasonable, would even be heard. And always, when the driver's request was refused, he would leave the bus and return shortly with a policeman and from then on the outcome was anybody's guess, depending on the policeman. Sometimes the policeman would suggest (if the passenger were white) that the driver just go on. Sometimes he would explain the law and ask the colored passenger to comply or get off, in which case he would usually ask the driver to refund the fare. In general, by tone of voice and manner, the policemen did try to give the appearance of calmness and reasonableness, but of course their very presence was an insult and always we ourselves found, though we knew it didn't "help" the passenger and possibly made it worse for him, that we couldn't be counted as approving by our silence, and must also protest.

"Yes," Ted said, as he pulled off his wet uniform and put his arm into the robe I was holding, "the same old thing, senseless and stupid as always—a colored soldier three seats from the back refusing to move to the back seat."

Barefoot, he followed me out to the kitchen and sat at the table while I moved between stove and table putting food before him. "Only this time," he said, "it wasn't a traffic cop the driver called in. It was two M.P.'s."

"For a state law?"

"That's the point I made," Ted said, "so they hemmed and hawed around and the M.P.'s asked the soldier's name and I said I thought he didn't have to give it and the soldier said he'd by God had enough and would rather walk and I could hardly ride, under the circumstances."

"You mean you walked twelve miles in the rain?"

"Yes. It was sort of like Gaston and Alphonse, the soldier's saying I didn't need to, and so on and so on. You can imagine. And then of course neither of us wanted to admit that the other one harmed his chances for a ride, so we just kept on, and the rain got harder. If white people in cars came by, they wouldn't stop for me because of him, and some colored soldiers came by, but when they saw me, of course, they didn't stop for him. Ow! What are you doing?"

"It's just soapsuds on a piece of cotton," I said. "I'm bathing the blister. Hold still. Well, anyhow, what about the colored soldier? In that distance you must have had plenty of time to get acquainted."

45

"No," Ted said, "we did just what any two strange guys do when they kill time together. We talked about baseball."

"*Baseball?*"

"Sure, baseball. What else? Got any more coffee?"

Ted had, thank God, one spare uniform home from the cleaners, and as I gathered up the soggy mess of clothing and tried to drape it around the kitchen where it might dry I wondered if the soldier's wife was also going through these same motions, hearing this same story.

"Sad thing is," Ted said, lighting a cigarette, "it wasn't just the colored-white thing. On top of it all, he was an enlisted man and I had the feeling he didn't really trust me because I was an officer."

"Well, anyhow," I said, throwing his wet socks into the trash basket, "you did me a favor. That sock on the blistered foot was one I mended. You convinced me it's no saving for me to mend socks. Now you've got to have an anti-tetanus shot."

"Oh, balls," he said. "A little blister on the heel. Ever since you had that nurse's aid course, you've been an alarmist."

"Say, you know what Mr. Hanna told me today? He's the one owns the hardware store, remember? Well, he said the creek has risen four feet. Everybody was down at the bridge tonight watching the water. It's all red from the mud and boiling and foamy. You ought to see it."

"Four feet?" he said. "Our fireplace must be gone, then. Were the people *on* the bridge?"

"Sure. Leaning over watching the water."

"You stay off the bridge," he said. "Look from someplace else."

"Who's an alarmist?" I said.

"I'm serious," he said. "I've seen all that creek from the air, remember, and what's more, that bridge is over a hundred years old."

So we made a bargain. He would see about the anti-tetanus shot and I would stay off the bridge.

46

"How's the score on Mrs. Emerson?" Ted said.

"Two more," I said. "Same thing. *Yes, indeed.*" I could not get Mrs. Emerson out of my mind and I had begun to ask people about her, but they would tell me nothing, until almost I thought I had made up the whole weird encounter. "I met Mrs. Emerson out on the Hester road," I said to Mr. Tibbs, the postmaster. He looked straight at me and said, "Yes, indeed." I waited. He didn't volunteer anything. Mrs. Roebuck, Mr. Hanna, the man who ran the movie, even Redley Stuart—all of them did exactly the same thing. They would look straight at me and then their faces would go blank and they would say "Yes, indeed." And nothing more. Taylor Frye had, after some thought, added, "Poor old thing," and then abruptly changed the subject. *Yes indeed* and *No indeed* made up about half the "white" conversation of Chinkapink, anyhow. It was sung, so:

No   in - deed!   Yes   in - deed!

"When you think what it must be like out there with all this rain," Ted said. "The roof surely hasn't been repaired in twenty-five years."

4

IT WASN'T ONLY old Mrs. Emerson that haunted me. Those two
semesters of "egg" required of boys who had neither interest nor
future in farming rankled around in the back of my mind until
I decided to speak to Mrs. Covington about it. How seriously,
in her judgment of the boy, could one take this wanting to be
an electrician, for example, and what plans had been made for
any education beyond this high school? Was there possibly some
information I could ferret out in a future trip to the city about
schools there? Serena was not in the store and I realized that I
had not seen her the day before, either.

"I miss Mrs. Covington," I said to Mr. Loftis. "Is she away?"

"No, Mrs. Demerest," he said. "She home. She feeling poorly.
I quite worried over her. She not one to . . . Well, you know
when she willin to lie down, she really sick."

"Oh, I am sorry," I said. "Would it be all right, do you suppose, if I dropped in to see her?"

His manner changed immediately to one of relief. "Why, that
be very nice," he said. "I'm sure she like that. It's just across the

street there. I wanted her to keep Sarah home with her, but she wouldn't have her miss school."

"You mean she's alone?" I asked, for I had never been in her house before and now I saw all kinds of complications. She might be taking a nap or have to get out of bed to let me in or it might embarrass her if the house were in disorder. As though he read all these things in my mind, Mr. Loftis began to walk with me to the door. "Now you just open the door," he said, "and call to her. She upstairs in bed. I be glad, Mrs. Demerest." He turned his face to me and I saw the great concern in it. "I be so glad if you would," he said.

"Well, of course," I said, "if you think . . . Well, all right."

Mr. Loftis continued to look over at Serena's house, his face marked with anxiety. "And how is the Captain?" he said, and then he turned and looked at me with—was it a look of conspiracy?

"Why, he's all right," I said, because it was probably only that I had read too many books about jungle telegraph systems. The soldier on the bus did not live in Chinkapink or Ted would have known of it. Surely Mr. Loftis had not heard. "He's getting lots of exercise," I said, and smiled up at him. Mr. Loftis smiled back and then we both began to laugh, and God knows, I thought, what we're laughing about, as I walked across the street and opened Mrs. Covington's front door quietly.

The living room was quite dark after the sunlight outside, but I could see that almost one whole wall was covered with plants. At the left I could see a large kitchen and on my right the stairway. The house smelled of Ivory soap and geraniums and, as with every house in Chinkapink, the sweetish smell of kerosene. At the foot of the stairs I called, softly, and Serena recognized my voice immediately and called out to me.

She seemed very much changed and it was obvious that she was quite ill. I sat down on a chair beside her bed and took her hand in mine. "I'm so sorry you're sick," I said. "I didn't know it until just now. Your father told me. What can I do for you?"

49

"You did enough," she said, "coming here. I feel much better just to see you."

I put my hand on her forehead; it was not hot, but damp with sweat. I took my handkerchief and wiped it off. It was cold in the house. "Would you like me to make you a cup of coffee?" I said. "And should I build up the fire?"

"Oh, no," she said, "I don't need anything. Papa been over this noon, and he wanted to fix a fire, but I told him I rather not have it. It worries me to be up here and have a fire downstairs that I can't watch." She closed her eyes and a white line appeared around her lips, so that I knew she was in pain, but she made no other sign.

"You cold?" she said.

"I have my coat on," I said. "I'm all right. But I'm worried about you. There isn't any doctor in Chinkapink, is there? Or dentist, or even a nurse?"

She smiled at me. "No," she said. "There's only Mr. Taylor Frye."

"Well, I suppose it does happen that people get sick here. What do they do?"

"Well, if they able, they go into Lawtonville," she said. "And then of course, if it's an accident or something, Mr. Taylor Frye have the ambulance."

"But if a baby's sick in the night, or something, isn't there someone they can call?"

"There's a doctor at the State Farm who comes for colored," she said. "He's a Frenchman."

"Well, can I . . . ?"

"Papa will call him," she said, "if the pain don't get better. Maybe the pain get better, so I could stand up, and then I could go into Lawtonville to the clinic."

"Well, of course, Mr. Loftis will know what to do. He was taking care of you long before I came here, I realize. I didn't mean to . . ."

"You just concerned," she said. "I appreciate it."

50

"Where is the pain?" I said. "I can see you're in pain."

"In my left side," she said. "It's not so bad now. Only if I try to stand up."

I waited and she did not volunteer any more information and what was the use of my banging questions at her if I could not relieve the pain? "Would you like me to get supper started?" I said.

"Oh, no," she said. "Sarah take care of everything when she gets home. Sarah a very good cook."

In short, there seemed to be nothing at all I was useful for and even my presence probably meant that she couldn't allow herself to groan when the pain hit. So I pushed my chair back and then I saw it, the pint whisky bottle hidden under the bed, and I looked away in embarrassment and got up to go.

"Was anybody in the store when you talkin to Papa?" she said.

"Why, no," I said. "Everybody's down at the creek all the time now watching the water. You must get well soon; you're missing all the excitement. Mr. Hanna runs over from the hardware store and measures the water every hour now."

"But why?" I said to Ted that night, for I couldn't get it off my mind. "Why should I be so all-fired upset about a whisky bottle?"

"You against whisky now?" he said.

"No, that's just the point. I don't have anything against whisky. Why should I have had that feeling of disappointment to see it there, like a little old W.C.T.U. member? If *I* were in pain like that I'd have a prescription for codeine in nothing flat, and a doctor and a warm house and a husband to make a fuss over me, so why should I begrudge her a little whisky?"

"I don't know," Ted said. "Hardly seems like you. But I hope you get all changed back again before I ever get sick. I . . . ."

"But that's *it*," I said, for I had suddenly seen myself solic-

51

itously carrying in a nice hot toddy to Ted in bed with a cold. "It wasn't the whisky at all."

"Probably you think I understand what you're talking about," Ted said.

"But don't you see, it's that it was *under the bed* that bothered me. If it had been on her bedside table, I wouldn't have thought a thing about it. It isn't like her to hide a bottle."

"Well, anyhow," he said, "it isn't like *you*, we know that for sure. Now can we go look at the creek?"

"Better look at the cellar first," I said. "By tomorrow I won't be able to get to the stove."

The water for the house was heated by a tiny wood-burning stove just seven inches in diameter, which was in the cellar, and we had both become extremely fond of it now that we had learned all its eccentricities. It did its job so well, really, for its size, and it roared so fiercely and made such joyous sounds, like a toy that has taken itself seriously. On Saturdays we would go to the woods to get fuel for it and then Ted would chop the wood into six-and-a-half-inch pieces and I would put them into paper sacks, eighteen pieces to a sack, and we would line all the sacks up for the week ahead in the kitchen, so that all I had to do when I needed hot water was to pick up a sack, go out the back door, enter the cellar (it had a real slanting cellar door), put the sack in the little monster, open the drafts, light a match, wait three or four minutes, close down the drafts and come upstairs. Twenty minutes later there would be enough hot water for washing dishes and running one full tub.

The Wilkies never went into the cellar at all and Ted said they were probably just so thrilled to have the water running out of a pipe that it hadn't occurred to them yet that there were further joys. But now not only was our wood supply low (it was too mucky to enjoy the woods) but the water had covered the cellar floor and was rising. So we managed a plank walk from one of the cellar stairs to the stove, and it was clear that if the water made this useless it would also make the stove useless. We got

52

pretty wet and cold before we were through and decided against going to see the creek. It was raining again when we went to bed.

In the middle of the night I suddenly awoke and sat up in bed.

"What-what?" Ted said. "What's the matter?"

"I am an idiot," I said. "I hate myself."

"Oh God," he said, "in the middle of the night? Can't you wait till morning?"

"No," I said, "I can't. Do you know what was really bothering me about that whisky bottle all the time?"

"Hidden," Ted muttered, sleepily.

"It just came to me, it was the wrong color for whisky. It was nothing but water. If you had a pain in your side and you didn't have a hot water bottle, what could be better? It's flat, it's small, and as the water cooled it would suck the cap on tight so it wouldn't leak."

"O.K.," he said. "You feel better now, then? We go to sleep now?"

"No, I feel worse," I said. "I've *got* a hot water bottle and she could have had the help of it all these hours."

"Jesus," Ted said. "Will you listen to that rain?"

As soon as Ted left for work next morning, I took the hot water bottle and a Thermos of orange juice to Mrs. Covington and for fear that if I were seen with them it might (in some way I did not understand) embarrass her, I carried them hidden under my raincoat. Her smile of greeting was warm and, it seemed to me, a little desperate, but this she quickly covered with her formality of the day before. She looked much worse, and I saw now that as she took the hot water bottle from me, the effort caused her arms to tremble. She lay back to rest herself for a moment, and once again I took my handkerchief and wiped her forehead. Yet I found a strong feeling of inhibition in the room which kept me silent and it was as though Serena and I were in some sort of contest, it being a question of which of us would break first, she to act from her pain or I to speak out my anxiety.

I saw signs of relaxation in her, as though the hot water bottle had produced some comfort, and, thinking she might sleep, I told her I would go and return in two hours to refill the bottle.

"I suppose you know all about the flood?" she said.

"No," I said, "I came straight here. I haven't been down to look yet."

"You mean you slept through it all?"

"I guess so," I said. "All what?"

"My land!" she said. "The whole town was up. People running around with lanterns and yelling. I thought it would never be morning so I could wake Joey up to go see. Why, the whole street is full of coffins. The water came up and covered the whole basement and the first floor of the funeral parlor. Joey say Mr. Taylor Frye just beside himself."

And so he was. The main street of the town from which the water had receded was an open account of the Frye enterprises. Fishing boats were piled against one another where some had been tossed and some dragged to safety. The ambulance was parked there and the fire truck and for half a block there were coffins stacked under tarpaulins or old quilts or any other kind of covering that could be found. Most of the other men had gone home to bed after being up all night and there were only a few people standing about in the fine drizzle, staring in a state of shock, while Taylor Frye, in hip boots, ran up and down nervously, unable to leave or rest or even accept.

"Look," he said to me, insisting that I bend down and inspect a coffin as he lifted the edge of a tarpaulin. "Look at that. Ruined. A coffin worth a thousand dollars, absolutely ruined. Look at that lining. Oh, it's awful."

Mr. Frye was nowhere in sight and I wondered when he had viewed the wreckage how he had answered greetings, for surely under such circumstances he had not said, "Very few people feel better than I do today. Very few people." Yet I had never heard him say anything else. I imagine that he went into a warm, dry place and read over his insurance policies and left the wringing of hands to Taylor. Taylor's distress was terrible to watch, and yet nobody believed in his loss, for everyone knew that nobody ever has a sale of damaged coffins, nor would these have their silver handles detached and be thrown on a junk heap. The people of Chinkapink would be buried in water-soaked coffins for a long time to come and they knew it. Jim Lawrence came now and put his arm around Taylor and said, "You come on, now, Mr. Taylor. I made you something hot to drink. Your clothes all wet. You gone have pneumonia." Jim's face had real sympathy in it.

I left them then, the two men standing in the drizzle among the symbols of death and pleasure, and it seemed the very essence of this tight, indrawn town that those of pleasure would be so simple (the rowboats were painted, if at all, in primary colors) and those of death so ornate.

5

ONCE IT HAD BEEN, if not exactly opposite, at least very different. This I learned from Mr. Loftis when I spoke to him in the store about the flood.

"The river used to bring such good to the town," he said, "and now seem like it only take away."

"Why," I said, "was it very different?"

"Oh, my, yes," he said, and even through his fatigue (for apparently he had been up all night helping in the flood, too) there showed a sparkle of excitement such as I had never seen him show before. "Oh, my, yes," he said. "This was a resort place long ago, did you know that?"

"I can't imagine it," I said. "What kind of resort?"

"Oh, people come from all over. Big boats came up Chinka-pink Creek in those days and famous people from all over would spend summers here. Two big hotels then, we had, and always full."

"Hotels?" I said, for I could not think of any building in the

56

town which could conceivably ever have been a hotel. "Where are they?"

"Oh, burned," he said. "This town been burned about completely out two times. The second time, the railroads already over at Hester, people didn't go by boat so much, and nobody just had the heart to start over, I guess. The dock burned completely the last time. Over there where Mr. Frye's place is now, there was a big dock, you know. Boats always comin and goin. Lots of people. Busy all the time. All the freight came by boat then."

"Was this store here, then?"

"Oh, my, no. I didn't even have a thought for this store then. I was a mate on a river boat. The captain, he taught me to count and I count the packages as we unload. But was they sardines or silk stockings, I couldn't tell because I couldn't read. Finally the captain, he taught me how to write my name, *Abel Loftis, Mt.*"

He reached over for a pencil and on a scrap of butcher paper wrote it for me. Pointing to the "Mt." he said, "That stand for mate on a river boat. That give me ten letters, you see, that belong to me. I had them."

And a lucky name it was, I thought, with all the vowels but one.

"Well, then," Mr. Loftis went on, "Mr. Hanna that has the hardware now, his father had a store here and I went to work for him. On Sundays, I used to make ice cream and sell it. There'd be people out walkin around, people takin boat rides, pleasurin theirselves. Ladies used to wear long dresses, then, and carry those little parasols. The hotels they be all lighted up in the evening, sometimes they had music. It all very nice, very busy. People run out of things on Sunday, you know. The store be closed and so I began to put in a few things like bread and some little things at my ice cream place. Well, then, one of the men say to me one day, 'Why don't you start a little store?' So I did. People just come in and take what they want. I never kept a record or anything. End of the month, they bring me some money. They were honest. I didn't lose by it. But the store kept growin and I kept onto my letters and I notice them, I watch for them. I try with the newspapers. Pretty soon I taught myself to read and write."

"To teach yourself," I said. "To think of it. It's a tremendous thing. I don't believe I could do it. I never met anyone who did that."

"Well, some things I do pretty good now," he said. "I get most the sense of everything on the front page of the paper. It take me quite a while, but I do it every day. And then, here in the store, I know everything in the store."

He walked out from behind the counter over to one of the shelves and began to move along, reading the labels. "Kleenex, Paper Napkins, Wheaties, Oatmeal, Post Toasties, Corn Flakes," he read.

"But it is wonderful," I said, "and of course to order you have to write them all, too."

"Yes," he said, "for the store, it pretty good. I know everything in the store, but . . ." He leaned over on the counter and sighed. With a sudden gesture of impatience, he jerked up his head and looked at me. "I know them," he said. "I call them. But . . . but I can't make them *go any place* or *do anything*, you understand."

"I understand," I said. "That's the kind of trouble I have with French."

"Those words," he said, "the ones that do things, that go places—they never come on a box so you can handle it over and over. Nobody ever ask for one. You don't sell it. I never gone get them now."

Surely, I thought, a man who could teach himself to read and write—even nouns alone—who could build a business that supported I don't know how many people, who could own a two-story house with a veranda, a man to whom many people came regularly for advice, a man who could do all that with four vowels, six consonants and a recipe for ice cream, surely he could

58

be trusted, without interference from me, to see that his own daughter did not die right in front of his eyes.

The next afternoon Mrs. Covington looked a little better. She was sitting up in bed.

"How are you today?" I said.

"Well, the doctor been here," she said. "The Frenchman from the State Farm."

"And what did he say?"

"Oh," she said, and as though she could not keep a straight face if she looked at me, she dropped her eyes to her hands. "He say maybe I have a cold and it settle in my side."

Oh, for God's sake, I thought. A diagnosis like that you can get by mail. But unless I were ready to offer something better, how would it serve her for me to destroy confidence in the Frenchman? "Well, at least," I said, "did he give you something for the pain?"

"Yes," she said, "he did, and it deaden it quite a lot. So now I can think better about what to do." She put one of her hands over mine and I saw then that mine were clasped tight in my effort to keep silence on the Frenchman. "I know how you feel," she said, "but I have to let Papa call him. Ever since my mother died, you know, Papa always blame himself she didn't have a doctor soon enough."

"Oh, then Miss Addie isn't your mother?"

"Oh, no," she said.

"I didn't think she could be," I said. "I wonder about it every time I see her."

"Because she so light?"

"Oh, that, and the gray eyes, I noticed of course. But it's more the . . . the personality, I guess. You're so warm, so . . ."

"She very unhappy woman. Seem to me she always was. I'm sorry for her now, now I'm older. I didn't think I ever could be."

"When you were little?" I said.

She laughed suddenly. "I don't think anybody ever had a

childhood like mine," she said, "but then I guess everyone feel like that."

"Everyone's probably right," I said. "Was there just John, your brother who's in the Army, and you, then, when your mother died?"

"Oh, no. I had a little sister named Evelyn. Evelyn's a nurse in New York City." A look of great pride came over Serena's face. "I show you a picture of Evelyn sometime. You like her. Evelyn a very nice person. She was a very sweet baby, too. Even Miss Addie like her. But John and me, she couldn't stand. When my mamma died, they taken us for a visit, John and Evelyn and me, and when we came home, why Papa was married to Miss Addie. We always call her Miss Addie.

"She taken a liking to Evelyn right off. Used to say Evelyn so sweet, so good. Used to say she couldn't understand how any child could be so bad, so unattractive as I was. Once she made Evelyn a whole doll's outfit—dresses, petticoats, panties, everything. I asked her would she make my doll just a dress. She said she was too busy.

"I used to get a whippin twice a day, every day of my life. And she didn't like John, either. One day it was snowing outside and Papa swept off the front porch so we could get some fresh air. She put us out on the porch and we wasn't supposed to go in because she scrubbed the floor. John he forgot and started in the house. She slam the front door on him so hard it knock him down and he slipped right off the porch and down the steps and he was unconscious. Papa came home and he bundled us up and took us all to Grandmother's in Lawtonville. Said he wouldn't leave us in the house overnight.

"While we there, Grandmother talk to us and she tell us maybe if we call Miss Addie mother, it makes her feel better toward us. So we came back and act as if nothin happen, but it wasn't any better.

"When I was eleven I went to work in people's houses and from that time on, I clothed myself. Miss Addie said she

60

wouldn't buy me clothes. Then she said she wouldn't wash any clothes for me either, or iron any. Of course Papa didn't know this. Papa didn't know but what he clothed me. We weren't allowed to carry tales. We weren't allowed to take the inside to the outside and we weren't allowed to carry tales from outside in the house.

"Then finally, Miss Addie said she wouldn't give me anything to eat. If Papa was home when I got home to lunch, then I would get to eat, but it seem like I always get home just before Papa or just after Papa had left. I got so I spent all the time I could at my aunt's. I don't know, if it hadn't been for her . . . She the only good thing I remember. When my aunt hear that Miss Addie said she wouldn't do any washing for me, she said, 'That's foolishness. If there's washing to be done, I'll do it.' Everybody's children were her children. I used to just *run* to her house and once I got inside that door, it was just peace. My aunt used to give me clothes and she used to tell me I did just grand. Always, every Sunday afternoon, my aunt would make cookies or candy or punch and we would all be there, getting to help, getting to put the cookies on the pan. And we would sing. We would all sit around and sing. My aunt loved singin and she said that we sang real good."

"Where is she now?" I said. You could use a little of that right now, I thought. "Is she living?"

"Oh, no," Serena said. "No. She dead. Lots of things might have been different if she had lived after we were all grown up."

"But didn't she ever speak to Mr. Loftis about the way things were for you at home?"

"No," she said. "It's a funny thing. I understand it, now. Papa was so good. Nobody could ever bear to tell him anything bad. Even yet, nobody can. John never could, either. Always, when I was little, my prayer every night, my wish every day, was that someday I could get to tell Papa what Miss Addie done to John and me. Last thing at night, every night, Papa always come in to tell us good night and put out the light and raise the window so we would have fresh air. Papa he always want everybody to have lots of fresh air. I used to lie there in the dark, achin and achin to tell him what it was like for John and me, but I couldn't."

"Oh, I can see," I said, "how neither you nor John could, but still, your aunt, I wish she might have . . ."

"Well, she did ask Papa, finally, could I come down and spend nights at her house. That was when Miss Addie tell Papa he have to take me out of school. She told him some boys had a house in the woods and that they taken me and Evelyn there. I didn't know hardly what she was talkin about then. People say where there smoke there's fire, but I never did find that house in the woods. I don't think it ever was. Anyhow, that was too much for my aunt. Then at my aunt's house I met a lady told me about a job as matron in a colored orphanage and asked me would I like to work there. I was crazy to do anything so I could get away. It was in Pennsylvania and I worked there four years.

"Meantime, Evelyn she got away to Lawtonville and lived with Grandma and she graduate from high school and she could get into a college if she had the tuition. Papa said he'd give half and I said I'd give half, so I sent the money home. Pretty soon I got a letter from Evelyn saying she would have to leave school because she hadn't paid her tuition. I borrowed the money and sent it to her.

"Then I got a letter from Papa saying could I please come home and take care of Miss Addie, that she seem to be morbid or something, couldn't take care of her children, he didn't know what to do. So I came. What could I do? Papa said the doctor say she must have something on her mind, but he couldn't find out what it was. 'It's Evelyn's money, that's what it is,' I said. We never did find it. That's the first Papa heard I sent it. I think Miss Addie didn't want the money, but she maybe tore the money order up in hate and afterwards surprised herself at what she did. Anyhow, she stopped being morbid and she would go on saying, 'Who told you? Just tell me who told you Evelyn didn't get her money?'

"Then she told Papa I never liked her, I always hated her, and Papa asked me about it. The devil must have got in me, then. I said, 'All right, Papa. You asked me. I been prayin. I been wishin for the day I could tell you. Now I'm going to.' Miss Addie was right there. 'I never wanted to tell anything behind your back,' I said to her, 'so I'm going to tell it all right in front of you.' So I told Papa everything—about the clothes, and the whippins and the food and the washing—about every mean thing. And Papa look so sad. He look so puzzled. 'Addie,' he said to her, 'is this true?' She just hang her head. 'Well,' Papa said, 'I guess silence gives consent. Silence gives consent, I guess. I don't see,' he said. 'I just don't see how I could live in this house all these years, right here with you, and not know. I thought I was clothin you,' he said. 'I thought I was feedin you. I thought she was treatin you good. Nobody ever said anything to me.'

"Oh, that I cut out my tongue before I ever said it," Serena said. Her eyes were closed and she put the back of one fist over them as though to shut out an unbearable picture. "I seen people die," she said. "I seen people fight. I never saw anything so scary as to see Papa that sad. He turn his back on us and he stand there a long time, his shoulders all crumple. 'Could that *be?*' he said. 'Could that be that little children cry theirself to sleep in a man's own house and him not *know?*' Oh, I should never, never have told him."

I reached out to touch her, not being sure of my voice. "It was all so long ago," I said. "It can't be helped. Sarah and Joey, they probably have regrets already. And I, so help me, I called my father a dirty old man and watched him cry not six months before he died. They've got these terrible things all over," I said. "It's people. It's being human causes it."

"He forgave you," she said.

"Who?"

"Your father. I sure he forgave you."

"Oh. Well, he did or he didn't, and what is it now? But anyhow, what did Mr. Loftis do? What did he say to *her?*"

"Oh," Serena said, "it scare her, too, to see him like that. For the first time she and I together on something. We feel like women together seein a man take on too much. After while Papa turn around. He not angry or cryin or anything. He just talk very quiet and he walk over to Miss Addie and he say, 'Well, you make it up to her now,' and then he walk out of the house and go in the store."

"And did she?" I said.

"Well, she try. I will say that. Pretty soon she take care of her children and do the housework and then she began to cook, so I could leave. I got married soon after that. We lived in New York and when my children born she came up to New York and stayed with me, and take care of my babies. I never see her kiss them. She never tell me they pretty or anything, but she bathe them, she wash diapers, she scrub her hands and be very careful of their belly buttons, just the way I ask. And she scrub my floor and get dinner for my husband. She wash my sheets. But she never a happy woman, you know. She never laugh in a happy way, not even with her own children."

Serena sat up a little straighter and ran her tongue over her lips. I got her a glass of water and after she'd drunk it she said, "My land! I don't know what you think of me, runnin on and on like that. It must be that pill I take loosen my tongue."

"It's about time you said something real to me," I said. "I was getting awfully tired of being treated like an ofay."

The laughter exploded out of her, so that she had to clutch her side in pain. *"Ofay?"* she said. "Oh, oh my, where did you learn a word like that? Not *down here?*"

"Oh no," I said. "Books, probably. You know me, always reading books. Why, did I say something bad?"

"No, it just so funny," she said, and she began to giggle. "It just so funny comin out of your mouth."

64

"You're making your side hurt," I said. "You'd better stop laughing. How often are you supposed to take these pills?" I reached for the box of codeine and saw written there *For pain, as needed,* and as I put it back on the bedside table, I suddenly had a hunch. "Serena," I said, "did you ever have pain like this before?"

"Oh yes," she said, "almost exactly, the pain and everything else, too. I had a growth on one ovary and I had to have it taken out about two years ago."

"Well, *all right,*" I said. "So let's do something sensible about it and stop all this hanky panky with the cold in the side."

"Oh, I know exactly what I have to do," she said. "I have to go to Lawtonville. There's a good clinic there for colored and doctors from the hospital come over to it."

"Fine," I said. "You want me to go with you?"

"*You?*" she said. "Well, land, no. I mean, that very kind . . ."

"O.K.," I said. "No. I heard you. Can I make the appointment for you?"

"There's no appointment," she said. "You just wait. I'll go," she said. "I know I got to go, but the thing is I got to be able to stand up, first."

"Why?"

"Because it most certain that the bus to Lawtonville be full and I'll have to stand. Now today I sit up. Tomorrow I stand. The next day I see can I make it."

"A bus?" I said. "You aren't able to get on a bus and it isn't necessary. Taylor Frye goes to Lawtonville every other day and he told me any time I wanted to go . . . I'm sure it will be . . ."

"Yes, Mr. Taylor Frye will take me," she said. "He do that as a regular thing for people here. But you understand one visit won't be it. First I go and see a general doctor. He very likely tell me when to come back to see a specialist. That's two trips. The specialist he maybe say I have to come again. Then if he gone operate it be a trip to the hospital. I have to figure pretty careful. Mr. Taylor, he charge five dollars a trip."

"Five dollars! Why, the bastard," I said. "It's only six miles and he has to go anyway. He takes me for nothing."

"Well, you his tenant," she said. "Now, no, no, Mrs. Demerest, please sit down. You too mad. You make me sorry I mention it at all."

"But it's outrageous. I can't wait to tell him what . . ."

"Now, Mrs. Demerest, you know he have to charge. You know perfectly well there's people in this town, white *and* colored, who be running into Lawtonville every time they out of thread if he didn't charge."

"Well, all right," I said, "that might be. So let him charge twenty-five cents. Or even fifty. But, my God, to ask five dollars of a sick person who's in pain. Oh, really, when I get through with him, if he has the nerve . . ." I started to put on my coat and, in my anger, I couldn't even find the armhole. "Of all the . . ."

And that fast, Serena was out of bed and on her feet and she got into the doorway, blocking it. "No," she said. "You gotta listen to me. Mrs. Demerest, you don't know. You gotta promise me . . ."

She was panting for breath and holding on to the door jamb and then she started to slump down, her face all gray. I caught her and held her head down and the two of us hobbled over to the bed somehow and I got her in it and, Christ, I was scared and there was no one, absolutely no one, to call.

"Serena," I said, "don't do that. Don't worry. All right, all right. I won't talk to Taylor, I promise. I promise anything until you get well. Whatever it is you want, so you won't worry."

"Could I have a little water?" she said, and after I had, half-spilling, given it to her, she said, "I'm sorry I scared you. I'm all right now. It just the pain, you know. But I had to stop you. I had to."

"Don't think about it again," I said. "Absolutely, I promise you, I'll put it out of my mind until after you're well and then

66

we can talk about it. I didn't know. I didn't know it would hurt *you* for me to give him hell. You want a pill now?"

"No," she said. "Thank you, but I save it for the night."

"Maybe I'd better take one," I said, for I was still shaking.

"You surprising strong," she said, "for your size."

When I saw that the color had returned to her face I decided I had done enough harm and I got ready to leave her. Sarah would be home in a few minutes, I knew.

"Mrs. Demerest," Serena said as I was leaving. "The Captain. Does he know you're here?"

"Ted? Why, of course," I said.

"And it all right with him?"

"Well, naturally, it's all right with him."

"You very lucky," she said, "to marry somebody like yourself."

I would never have said Ted and I were alike. There was one thing, though, now that I thought about it, and that was that Ted and I would each have thought Mrs. Covington's remark a compliment—I because it lent me dignity and he because it gave him spirit.

6

THE FLOOD, which had been so hard on Taylor Frye, turned out to be a great boon to me, for when the paths in the woods became once again walkable, they were heaped with small pieces of wood six inches long, one-and-a-half inches in diameter, and perfectly straight. I never found out what kind of tree they came from; they had apparently been washed from high in the surrounding hills. The length of the pieces, I suppose, represented the interval of branching, and their uniformity of size no doubt meant a gradation of the water's sifting out by weight. The bark, when wet, was black, and on drying became a speckled gray. We called them fagots, for Ted teased me about being, at heart, one of those old women in paintings who search the woods for fagots to burn or sell. "It makes me feel less like a tourist," I told him, "to go to the woods *for* something."

The abundance meant for me, in addition to an easy fuel supply for the little monster, many bonus factors, for such is the perversity of a mind like mine that if I went to the woods to think about a story my mind would be a blank, but if I were gathering wood stories would mutter among themselves just under the surface and fight to get out first. The discovery of the wintergreen and all the new plants I learned was, in almost every case, incidental to some other thing and never when I deliberately sought them.

Moreover, I had now this elegant sack in which to gather the wood. One of the most maddening things to me about our civilization is the way we all refuse to admit that we are ever going to be laden, when the truth is we are constantly laden. All the years in school I could remember slipping, dropping books that were inadequately held up by protruding stomachs and bizarrely placed hip bones, because only sissies were supposed to carry satchels. The design of women's handbags, the pockets in men's suits, the oranges and potatoes and bottles of milk that regularly work their way out of the bottoms of paper sacks on the way home from the grocery—all these keep on insisting, in the face of the facts, that behind each of us as we go out there trails a nonexistent retinue of servants to carry. And while we bulge and joggle and struggle, we see the postcards, the travel posters, the movies of Tahiti and Mexico, and the most prominent things in them, always, are the baskets, the easy, expansible, beautiful baskets. Which, of course, we buy the minute we get to Tahiti or Mexico and bring home to set them by the fireplace to hold the kindling, the knitting, the magazines. Ah, those baskets, so used to voyaging, they never voyage any more. *We* voyage. Closing the door on the room that holds the basket, we go forth, laden, bulging and struggling, never admitting but what this is only a momentary or temporary condition.

I, too, of course, the very next time I went with Taylor Frye to Lawtonville, would perpetuate this foolishness. But not in the woods, not gathering fagots. For once in Mr. Loftis' store I had seen an empty mesh bag of woven rust and gold string. "What beautiful colors," I said to Mr. Loftis. "You like to have one, Mrs. Demerest?" he said. "They nice and clean." And he went into the back room to get me one. When I turned it over it said,

69

CARL KRUMMREY MICHIGAN ONIONS MC GUFFEY, OHIO and inwardly I was convulsed to find myself thinking: *A Yankee sack, so nice and bright.*

So, on my first trip after the flood, I took the fagot sack out of my pocket and began to gather the unbelievably uniform fagots and so I discovered the bustling mass of scurrying, disinherited creatures. Everything that is usually under something was now on top—bugs, beetles, baby mice, baby squirrels, even worms. All of us busy homemakers were carefully picking our ways over dislocated rocks and ground-up leaves and roots, hunting, hunting, for the domestically useful. I saw a giant spider, egg sac hanging, trying to negotiate her way across a splinter which bridged a puddle. "You babies draggin the bridge," I said to her, and, as though she heard me, she arched her back and retracted the egg sac closer to her abdomen.

I've got to quit that, I thought. I have to stop talking colored. I'm going to do it before Mrs. Covington someday and she'll think it's deliberate. I was, by now, well aware of the curse of living in a world primarily auditory and of how one's husband could be condemned to finding himself living successively with Garbo, Katharine Hepburn or Margaret Mead. In a way I was not so very different from Mrs. Wilkie, except that, with me, it happened unconsciously, while she, I assumed, strove for her imitations. In Chinkapink I could not use the usual remedy to jar me loose from colored talk, to substitute a new imitation by going to see a movie. The movie we couldn't stomach again.

One night we had asked Joey if he'd like to go to the movie with us and he had gone home for permission, which was granted. The "movie" was an old barn on the outside, next door to the old mill which no longer functioned. Like everything else, it was on the main street. As soon as we stepped out of the alley onto the street, Joey left us and ran ahead. Soon he came back. "Captain Demerest," he said, "could I buy the tickets? I hurry on and bring them back to you." As soon as our tickets

70

and the change were in Ted's hand, Joey flashed away, calling, "I'll see you after the show, at your house."

It seemed incredible now that we hadn't anticipated the situation, but neither of us had thought of it at all and once inside we saw only white people around us. Finally in the dark, just under the ceiling in the rear of the building, so close to the roof that there could not have been standing room, we saw the makeshift "balcony" for the colored patrons. There were no improvements or decorations inside the building. If we had thought of the problem at all, we would have assumed that, since they had done nothing else to the barn, they wouldn't have gone to this ridiculous length to build a balcony where there wasn't space for one. Outside the theater, there was no sign of Joey, but when we got home he was sitting on the steps. "I beat you home," he said.

So I wouldn't get any help on my cursedly imitative speech from the movies. I would just have to watch it. I threw the bag of fagots over my shoulder and picked my way over the rubble toward home.

The rest of that day, when I recall it, is all in bits and pieces. I know that on the way home I stopped at the post office. I was in Roebuck's Grocery, too, but I don't know if that was before or after I saw Mrs. Covington. And, yes, I went to Hanna's Hardware, too, for the washboard. Ted took the regular laundry into the Fort, but of course there were always some things that were too fragile to send there, or things we couldn't wait a week for, and as these got gradually dingier I had come to the conclusion that I needed a small hand washboard. This being wartime, the board had no metal on it, the ridges being cut into the wood, and, as with practically everything else shoddy and ersatz, it was called VICTORY in bright red letters written across the soap rest. As always, I remember, this infuriated me. Who in Christ's name is it, I thought, who has the power to convince millions of people that they can't face unpleasant facts, and goes around lousing up the language like this so that, for years now, a

71

good strong word like victory will really mean *inferior,* and sensible planning will become *sacrifice* and noble deaths will be turned into foolish *passings away?* Why can't they just say: *This is a necessarily lousy washboard at this time?*

Anyhow, I remember that I dropped the fagots at the kitchen door and lit the kerosene stove before I'd taken my sweater off. While the coffee water was heating (it was an indulgence, as low as the supply was, almost as if I had known in advance) I put a few things to soak in suds and then I carried the mail into the living room. Ted always opens his mail in the post office and walks along reading while things fall out of the envelopes, and he is very impressed at the way that I can put mail down unopened until I have the coffee and comfortable chair to go with it, but I tried long ago to explain to him that it is not strength of character really, but only a measure of a person who has lived a long time alone and has consciously elevated many routine things into pleasures. He was even more impressed, though, when he learned that I always left his love letters unopened until I had had a bath and combed my hair and put on perfume.

When I carried the coffee into the living room and sat down by the red-linen-covered footlocker, I could not help but glow a little at the room after the great disorder of the flooded woods. It was so pleasant now, with the soft light of the new lamp picking out the blue of Ted's tobacco can, the golden crust of Vermeer's bread, the stone jug filled with red and gold leaves. So I read the mail and in it was the news of our old friend Larry's having been killed in flight training, the first of our friends to become a war casualty. It was too much like Larry's life, this death, not even to have made it to combat, but to have died by somebody's accidental bungling. It was all too pat, like the plot of a bad novel.

I could remember the night of the last party and how another friend, Louis, had somehow been possessed, so that he began, like a small boy playing at war, to go on and on and on at Larry about a new design for a bayonet with a hook that could be released from

72

the handle into the guts. When I had missed Larry later I had found him lying in the dark bedroom, alone, blind with migraine (having, as always, carefully tidied up after himself in the bathroom—the only one of the whole gang who ever did). And I had sat down on a chair in the dark room near the bed while he wailed at me: "Christ, Molly, will you tell me why I let him needle me like that? Honestly," he said, "what the hell am I going to do? The most sublime, the most beautiful, heroic or terrible thing could happen to me and I've got but one reaction—no matter what. I vomit. What'll I do?" he said. "I can't vomit my way through a whole war."

Well, now he wouldn't, I guess. Not any more.

Our room, when I looked up from the letter, was transformed into as mocking and foolish a thing as the very ersatz language I had been so angered about, for wasn't it a ridiculous play-acting to have a "home" in homeless times, weren't these "roots" garishly theatrical? Would we really not have been more comfortable in a comfortless place? Oh, today, yes, of course. Maddening to think that when the very curtains were being hemmed with the easy-to-take-out bastings, Larry was already surely, even then, dead. But tomorrow would it seem again, this place, a refuge or a silly gesture?

The coffee was cold and I took it out to the kitchen. While I was there, I lifted a nightgown out of the soapsuds and moved it across the new washboard a couple of times. And the red VICTORY ran, of course, all over it. Damn such people who will put on a washboard something that won't stand water, I thought, and I hurriedly put the streaked nightgown under the faucet, hoping to salvage it. Suddenly I was leaning over the sink crying into the suds and so real were they all to me then, the gang, that I turned the faucet the way that would have been right in the old place, but was wrong here. A great splash of water spilled all over me and onto the floor before I got it turned off. I wiped my eyes and blew my nose on the dish towel and got the mop from the back porch and "Oh, God," I said, "I forgot about

Mrs. Covington." For she had gone, that day, with Taylor Frye to the clinic in Lawtonville and I had meant to be there to meet her when she got home.

As I rounded the corner by Serena's house, two colored women came out and walked toward me and one said, "Poor Serena, she gone lose her bedroom furniture." The other one giggled nervously and said, "Oh, my, I'm glad I ain't gone lose *my* bedroom furniture." "Me neither," the first one said. "I think if I Serena I'd argue some with that doctor. I say, *Doctor, you take de dresser. You take de commode. You take de bedspread and de mattress, but leave me dat bed.* Oh, good evenin, Mrs. Demerest," she said. "I dint see you."

"Evening," I said, as I walked by them. Damn their eyes. Oh, what a cursed day this had been. Fifteen minutes sooner and I might have been able to forestall this. It was exactly the reason I had wanted to be there, exactly what I had wanted to protect her from. The harm had been done now; there was no need to burst in on her out of breath. I walked as slowly as I could to the door. Serena was downstairs, sitting in a chair.

I walked over and put my arm around her. "Was it a rough trip?" I said. "I'll bet you're tired."

"Well, some," she said, "but not bad."

"You saw the doctor?"

"Yes," she said, "and the surgeon happen to be there today so I saved a trip."

"That's good," I said. I lighted a cigarette and hunted around till I found an ashtray. "Well?" I said.

"He say I have a growth on the womb," she said, "and I have to have an operation to remove it."

"The growth?"

"Everything." She looked at me, that clear, level look she had, that made things no worse than they were and no better, either.

"Do you need money?" I said. "I'm sure Ted . . ."

"Oh, no," she said. "That very thoughtful of you. I'll go to

74

the bank tomorrow and see how things are. Then I let you know."

"When do you think you'll go to the hospital?"

"The doctor he wanted me to go right away but I can't get in for two weeks. The hospital full."

Well, what was I waiting for? Had I expected her to say, "I have a fear that measures six on the fear index. It is such and such a shape, this fear, and such and such a size?" And if she had, what was it I had to offer? *You call it a tumor of the uterus, honey. That's not anywheres near as bad as a growth on the womb.*

"If you'd trust me with your stove," I said, "I'd make you a cup of tea. You ought to have something."

"Why, there's some made," she said. "Fedora fix it before she left here. The cups right on the table there."

I wish Fedora had fallen in the pot and drowned, I thought, before she opened her big mouth. I got us each a cup and carried it into the living room. Mrs. Covington sat, in deep thought, staring at the toe of her shoe.

"I expect you'd like to lie down," I said. "Can I help you upstairs before I go?"

"Oh," she said, "while I'm here, I think I'll just stay till after the children get home. It make them feel safer to see me sit up."

"I've been wanting to ask you about Joey—his wanting to be an electrician. How serious do you think it is? He's so disgusted with that stupid agriculture class, I thought maybe I could encourage him about getting books on electricity and locating schools if you thought it was a real interest."

As I had hoped, this did distract her from her preoccupation, and she gave me a smile of great tenderness. "I don't know how serious it is," she said, "but I know where it came from, all right. Joey and I were over at a friend's house and her radio wouldn't work. Joey said he thought he could fix it and she said not to touch it, that her son would be home soon and he'd fix it. She was afraid Joey would break it. Well, time came for her favorite program and her son still hadn't come, so finally she said Joey could try. She wanted to hear that program so bad, she'd risk it. So Joey he did something to some wires and turned the radio on and it worked fine. Everybody, you know, like to have a success." Then she frowned. "Why, that been seven or eight months ago," she said. "I'll have to see to it that Joey have another success right away soon now."

"I noticed," I said, "how careful Mr. Loftis is to compliment Joey on the jobs he does around the store."

"Oh yes, Papa," she said. "Well, that's the whole thing, of course. I don't know. I don't know if I did right or not. You see, if I had stayed in the North when my husband died, the children would have had better schools. I knew that, but I had to go to work and leave them alone. So I had to decide which was more important, the school or the home. You see, here I can own property. I own this house. The bank trust Papa and if Papa give his name, the bank here lend you money."

"And then there's Mr. Loftis himself," I said, "for the children to know while they're growing up. To have a grandfather so respected by everybody, you'd have a hard time finding anything to equal that for an advantage."

"Well, that was it," she said. "I thought, which is better—a good education with your mamma working, and living in a rented place, or a bad education where you live in your own house and know someone like Papa. I don't know did I make the right decision or not."

"You shouldn't have had to make such a choice," I said. "They should have been able to have Mr. Loftis *and* a good school."

"I hope the children feel I did right," she said, "but I don't know. Sarah now, she worried. A girl graduated last year and when she tried to go to college, they wouldn't take her credits. Said this not an accredited school."

"Oh oh, that's really rough," I said.

"Poor Sarah, she make all A's, you know. She smart and she

76

knows it silly to waste her time. Like that art class. One whole semester they spent folding crepe paper to make those things you hang around the room Christmas time. They must have enough of them to decorate ever house in Chinkapink. Course it's not the teacher's fault. Crepe paper happen to be all she got."

"It's wicked," I said. "But at least we can find out about the college ahead of time so Sarah doesn't have to wait until she tries to enter to find out the requirements."

"That would be good to do," Serena said. "Sarah pretty bitter already. She say with her own children she'll turn Catholic."

"Oh?"

"That way, you do get the education and the high Catholic school got to take from the low Catholic school."

"Yes," I said, "the Protestants really missed the boat on that one. They had the same chance to take a stand and to guarantee an education, and they missed it."

"Well, the Protestants, you know, they all got to agree before they can ever act."

"There's the school bus," I said. "I'll see you tomorrow and . . . well . . ." Greeting card firms keep boasting they cover all situations, I thought. I wonder if I could get one that says *So sorry about your womb* and send it to her in the mail? I sure as hell couldn't say it. So I bent to kiss her forehead instead.

"Mrs. Demerest," Serena said, "it's a good surgeon. I'm satisfied of that. He on the staff of the biggest white hospital and I know other people he taken care of. He taken great care to explain everything to me and I know it has to be done for my own good."

That was the night Taylor Frye brought me the new, gleaming white toilet seat to replace the miserable splintery mahogany one of which I had so long complained.

"And did you keep your promise?" Ted said when he saw it.

"Not to say anything about the five dollars he charges Mrs. Covington for transportation?"

"Yes, I did," I said, "with great difficulty."

"I want you to know," he said, "I don't underestimate the difficulty. Especially today."

"That's praise, I take it," I said.

"Yes, indeed," Ted said. "If Taylor Frye lives to be a hundred, I don't imagine he'll ever come so close to having a toilet seat busted over his head."

"You read the mail, I guess?"

"Yes," he said, "and I saw the washboard and the nightgown and the mop. Pretty lousy day all around, you had."

"Wait till you see dinner," I said. "It's really disorganized."

"The hell with it," he said. "You have cheese and crackers or something we could take to the woods?"

The woods. Yes, that was the right thing to do, the right place to go when your friends get killed in a routine training flight or contemplate serious surgery. "Our fireplace is gone," I said. "I was there today getting fagots."

"We'll build a new one," he said. "Did Mrs. Covington seem very much afraid of the operation?"

"I suppose she is," I said, "but now that you ask, well no, it doesn't seem like fear. More . . . sad. She seems very sad. I don't know what it is, really, but . . . Why, I've *seen* her afraid. When she thought I was going to talk to Taylor Frye about the five-dollar charge, that's when she was afraid. This isn't fear. It's something else, something I don't understand yet."

But I had seen fear that day, surely, or was it the day before? I had certainly seen fear that had made a real impression on me, and where was it?

In the woods we sat on a blanket around a small makeshift fire. Our bread and cheese finished, we smoked cigarettes and heard how different, at a distance, the creek sounded. Usually when we had a fire in the woods, our ears would be so filled with the roar of the water we couldn't speak together at all. Now, since the flood, the only relatively firm place was far removed. Also, the creek had grown wide and more placid, fat with red mud and leaves, logs and rocks. It was better, for this day, to be in a quieter place while the hectic pieces of the day fell into some order. And *that* was it. In the confusion of the day's events it had quite slipped my mind that I had been in Roebuck's Grocery and that it was there, on Mrs. Roebuck's face, that I had seen such fear.

"Why, Ted," I said, "I almost forgot. I saw Mrs. Emerson today, at last, and you can quit worrying if she drowned in the flood. She was in Roebuck's Grocery and what I mean is, she had them all at her mercy. Mrs. Roebuck is afraid of her."

"How do you know?"

"She told me so, for one thing. But she didn't need to. The store was full of people and Mrs. Emerson sat up at the front in the window with her back to the light. You couldn't see her face well, but she could see everybody in the store. Mrs. Roebuck was trying to wait on people and she got more and more nervous. She kept spilling things and dropping things. And with Lizzie Benoit gone, there isn't anyone to ride herd on Lou Ann, you know. She was into everything and Mrs. Roebuck was screaming at her and trying to catch her, but of course Lou Ann can run faster than anything (poor Lizzie runs all day long after her) and the ladies waiting to be waited on would giggle nervously about Mrs. Emerson and forget what they wanted. But I tell you, old Mrs. Emerson knew it and I'll swear, she was enjoying it. 'I'd like some *ice* cream, Mrs. Roebuck, if you please.' And Mrs. Roebuck would drop everything and take her a little carton of ice cream. '*And* a wooden spoon, if you please,' Mrs. Emerson would say, and Mrs. Roebuck would trot up to the front of the store with the spoon. And then Mrs. Emerson would say, 'And *here* is your five cents, Mrs. Roebuck,' holding out a nickel in one of those claws of hers, and 'Yes, Mrs. Emerson,' Mrs. Roebuck would say, trotting up to take the nickel. The old woman sat there in full view of everybody, slowly, slowly eating her ice cream and staring the ladies down when they looked at her. One of the women saw me there and she put her finger up to her temple and circled it in explanation to me and giggled, you know, the way people do, so I said to her, quietly, 'Well, what about her, do you know? Who cares for her?' And the woman stopped giggling and suddenly gave me that blank look and said . . ."

"Yes indeed," Ted sang.

"That's right. I tried several of them at the back of the store while I was waiting and got the same thing from all of them. I hated for Mrs. Emerson to think I was one of them and I wanted to leave, but I knew that would make Mrs. Roebuck think I was sore at not getting waited on. She kept apologizing, each time she'd trot by me (I've never seen the store so full), and once she said, 'Poor crazy old thing. I'd like to get her out of here, but to tell you the truth, I'm afraid of her.' "

"Did Mrs. Emerson know you?"

"No. I went up to her and spoke to her. She didn't know me. She gave me a very condescending bow of the head, quite formal, and said: 'It's always an experience, seeing the Chinkapink ladies. They get an idea and they're so reluctant to part with it.' "

"I'll bet she's right at that," Ted said. "You know, I feel sorry for that little Roebuck girl. Nobody ever does anything but chase her. And she's so pretty and so smart."

"That's Lou Ann's trouble," I said. "She is so smart and nothing to do with it. She's the kind of child that would really profit from a good nursery school and lots of stimulation from other children."

"Don't they even have a kindergarten here?"

"I'm not sure, but even if they do, she's too young. She's only four years old."

"Only four? But her talk is so grown-up."

"Oh, you don't know how grown-up," I said. "The other day in the store she asked me where my daddy was (that's you; all men are daddies) and I said you were at work and she said in a loud voice, 'Say, what does your daddy *do* to you when he gets you in bed at night?' "

"In the *store?*" Ted said. "She asked you that in the store?"

"And it was so quiet you could hear the ladies breathing while they waited for me to answer."

"And what did you find to say?"

"Oh, I said you told me bedtime stories. Beautiful bedtime stories."

"What presence of mind," Ted said. He put his arms around me and kissed me. "There is that one, you know," he muttered into my ear, "about the big bad wolf and . . ."

"And," I muttered in *his* ear, "the one about the people who forgot to pull down the shades."

"Remind me," he said, "remind me. But what in the world is a four-year-old doing *up* that late?"

"I don't know," I said, "but how would she ever get normally played out like other children? She doesn't have anyone to play with."

"That's right," he said. "The Wilkie children are the only white children I've seen. Come to think of it, I haven't seen many white people young enough to have children her age."

7

AND WE WEREN'T to see the Wilkie children much longer, for a few days later Mrs. Wilkie loaded Gary Cooper, Rita Hayworth and Joan Crawford into a taxi and went away. But she did not, alas, take her towel with her. And as a memento, it grew constantly more fragrant.

"This thing is getting to be an obsession with me," I said to Ted. "Now that Mrs. Wilkie and the kiddies are gone, and with the new white toilet seat, the place is really sparkling and easy to keep that way. It looks so nice. You enter. And, God, it gags you."

"Yes," he said, "it is getting pretty high, all right."

"What do you suppose would happen if I just burned that rag," I said, "and furnished Wilkie with a clean towel every day?"

"Oh, I don't know," Ted said. "That's a pretty personal thing, a towel. I suppose he'd get insulted and sore."

"Well, I can't ignore it. I've tried and I just can't control my feelings about it. I can't forget it. Why, I keep having imaginary conversations with Wilkie all day long."

"With *Wilkie?*"

"Yes," I said. "Sometimes I'm righteous. I give him what for and I call him a filthy pig and if he doesn't get that stinking towel out of here, I'll . . . so on and so forth. Then other times I try the Girl Scout approach. 'Now, Mr. Wilkie, you'll have to help me keep things clean around here. Let's co-operate.' And then sometimes I think the woman line would go down better: 'I know how men are. With your wife gone and all, you just forget. I'll take care of it. It's a *woman's* job.' "

"All this over a rag of a towel?" Ted said. "Well, tell me, in your imaginary conversations, when you try out these lines on Wilkie, what does Wilkie answer?"

"That's the trouble," I said. "He never says anything at all. I cannot imagine a single line for him."

I certainly couldn't have imagined the line Wilkie did say the next day. He had changed to the day shift at the State Farm, and, as I was taking some things down from the clothesline, he came up to me. "Evenin, Mrs. Demerest," he said.

Now, I thought, is surely going to be my chance and quick, quick, which shall it be—indignant, Girl Scout, the woman thing?

"Would yall ask the Lieutenant to wake me up in the mornin?"

"Oh?" I said, thinking *Sure I will, if you'll get rid of that stinking towel.* "What time?"

"He gets up about seven, don't he?"

"Yes," I said. "But if your alarm's broken" (there were none for sale in Chinkapink; we had found out the hard way) "and you need to get up earlier, you could borrow ours."

"Nope," he said. "Alarm clock just don't do me no good. Nevah heah it. Ahv trahd everything. Put the alarm in the dishpan, set it raht by ma head. Nevah heah it. Now you tell the Lieutenant just to come on in and turn on the light. Sometimes that'll do it. It shines raht in ma eyes. But if that don't, you tell him just to hit me on the chest. I gotta get up in the mornin," he said. "Ahm gonna lose ma job. Ahv overslept now three days in a row. You tell him now, heah? Don't knock, tell him. Ah won't heah it. Just come on in and turn on the light and if Ah don't answer, hit me on the chest."

"Well," I said, "I'll ask him. . . ."

"Don't you forget, heah?"

There I stood at the clothesline, so completely flabbergasted that I hadn't even had a chance about the towel for thinking what unpleasantness I had got Ted into. Because Wilkie couldn't possibly have made a worse choice in asking someone to invade his privacy. Ted was the man who had suffered insomnia all through basic training because there were sixty-nine other men in the room where he was supposed to sleep. He had, of course, had to make some adjustments since then. Dead from lack of sleep, he had finally got to be a p.f.c. and even a corporal, where he had wangled some kind of quarters so there were only nineteen other men in the same room. He had even been able to choose one half of a tourist cabin instead of a park bench in a town where these were the only alternatives the day we hit it, and, with not too great a sigh of relief, he had good-humoredly helped the tenants of the other half hang a blanket over an improvised clothesline between the two beds. He had even fallen asleep, at last, in that bed. I remember next morning, after the two men had gone off to the camp, as the other woman and I were trying to make coffee over canned heat set between two rocks, she had said to me, gushingly, "Oh, I do hope you stay. You don't know how much it means to have somebody refined in that other bed. The last couple, my goodness . . ." "Honey," I had said to her, "we aren't refined. We're self-conscious."

But, even so, as many adjustments as Ted had made, the idea of going into a stranger's bedroom while he was asleep and touching him . . .

84

"Well, I didn't say you'd do it," I said to him that evening. "I said I'd ask you."

"I don't suppose it would kill me," he said. "One morning."

So the next morning he knocked at the door and called, "Seven o'clock, Mr. Wilkie," and nothing happened, so he went in and, wincing, turned the light on in the man's eyes, and nothing happened, and so then, hesitantly, he reached out and made himself touch the man.

"And my God," he said to me, "he damned near strangled me." He was sitting at the breakfast table and he was still breathing hard, still red in the face, from having had to fight off Wilkie. "Why, he's terrified," Ted said. "He's afraid for his life. He was in the air and had me by the throat before I even knew what happened. I had an awful time getting him loose. I had to throw him on the bed. All this, you understand, was with his eyes closed. Then he opened his eyes and said, 'Mornin, Lieutenant. Thanks for wakin me up.'"

"Well, you can't go through that every morning," I said.

"Oh, I'll have sense enough to step out of the way next time," Ted said. "I didn't know what was coming. I never saw anything like it. Do you suppose they'd let someone in that condition carry a gun at the prison?"

"I don't know," I said. "He doesn't wear it home, though. You want me to ask him?"

"You stay away from him," Ted said.

Mrs. Covington was sitting up most afternoons now when I dropped in to see her. She had a wood stove in her living room and she would sit by it in a rocking chair, looking out the window often at her garden. She never had knitting or fancywork of any kind and I rarely found her reading. Usually she was just sitting, her hands quiet in her lap. She was always glad to see me, always sparkled a little bit, and then she would lapse into quiet spells in some withdrawn place. She had a look of sadness, often, a kind of resignation in her posture. She was not agitated, did not appear to be afraid. You could hardly even call it sadness. It was just that she was preoccupied.

"Is it the money?" I said. "Are you worried about money?"

"No," she said. "I've been to the bank. The doctor gone charge me fifty dollars and the hospital sixty-four. I own this house, you know, and I've borrowed on the house so I can leave the hospital all clear. Nothing drive me crazy like bills. Now, it all taken care of. Of course, John left his money with me when he went to the Army and I have that, but I couldn't use John's money."

"Well, perhaps it's the children," I said. "Are you satisfied in your mind about the children?"

"Well, no," she said. "I guess the best thing is for them to stay here. Sarah, you know, is fifteen. She perfectly competent to take care of them and to keep the house."

"I know she is," I said, "but still, people in a hospital sometimes worry anyhow. Wouldn't you feel better if there were an older person in charge?"

"Well, some ways yes and some ways no. You see, I can't ask Miss Addie. I can't send them over to Papa's. And if I ask any other colored woman to come here, it . . . it look like a slap at Miss Addie before everybody."

"I can understand that," I said. "But how about me?"

"You?"

"Yes, me. You'd trust me, wouldn't you? The children can stay with us or I'll come up here."

"Well, no, that wouldn't be necessary, Mrs. Demerest, and that awfully kind of you. But you give me an idea. You see, it really is best all around if the children stay right here. The only thing I would have on my mind would be Joey, he's at the age to tease. And Sarah, she's just at the age she take teasin hard and sometimes she get out of patience with Joey and they scuffle some. You know, it's nothin—just brother-sister things—when I'm here to make Joey stop his teasin. But in the hospital, I would get to thinkin if they were in the kitchen and the kero-

86

sene stove there and all. Now, if I tell them *you* gone be checking up on them, then Joey be like an angel. Joey, he wouldn't have you criticize him for anything. And if Joey on his best behavior, Sarah will be. You don't need to do anything at all. Just let me tell them you *might* be by to see if they're behavin."

Privately I thought I could do a little better than that, but the thing now was not to make her anxious about inconveniencing *me*, not to make her regret that, for once, she had been able to ask something, however small, of me. "Of course," I said. "And then there's always your father right across the street."

"Oh, yes," she said. "Papa. Underneath, at the bottom of everything, there's Papa." She smiled and rocked back and forth in her chair. She looked out the window where the late afternoon light was lying so golden on the last few chrysanthemums. "I always loved autumn the best," she said, "but this year . . ."

Well, we had gone over the money and the children and we hadn't touched what caused the preoccupation. "Have you written to your sister in New York—the nurse—about going into the hospital?" I said.

"Evelyn? Well, no, I haven't yet."

"I just thought," I said, "if there's anything bothering you about it, maybe you could ask her and she could probably reassure you."

"I'm not worried about the operation, Mrs. Demerest."

"I know," I said. "You told me that already. And I believe you. You don't act like someone who's afraid, anyhow. You act like someone who's sad."

"Ah," she said.

"It's rubbing off on me," I said. "I can feel it so strong. I go around feeling sad and I don't know what I'm sad about."

"I'm sorry for that," she said. "I didn't mean for you to notice. It's just . . . just that I have to make up my mind to do something, now, and every day the time gets shorter."

I reached out and took her hand and, surely, why should she

87

tell me, I thought. What makes me so confident that I could help her with it, this decision, if I knew what it was?

"Well, I'll tell you," she said, looking then directly into my eyes. A slow smile came into her face. "You see, I had thought quite a lot of getting married again. There is this man I met when I worked for a while up in Lawtonville, and he wants me to marry him. . . ."

"There is!" I said. "I'm so glad you told me. You know, I've worried about that. It seems to me, you're so much more than most people a . . . a loving person. You give it out so, and I didn't think two children, even such nice children, were enough. I thought you must be very lonely."

"Well, several times I've started to tell you," she said. "One day you came and I'd just got a letter from him. It had a lot of pictures in it and I started to show them to you, but I thought that's childish, so I didn't."

"What's his name?"

"Devereaux," she said. "Albert Devereaux. He's in the Army. He's never seen the children but he said he want them to take his name if we get married. He said if it couldn't be done just like that, then he like to adopt them so they know he be responsible and so he could feel like he had two children. But now . . ." The happiness suddenly left her face and sadness crept over it again, slowly. "You see, he's tryin to get a furlough and he wanted to come here for me to marry him then, right away. I wanted him to come here. I wanted for Papa to see him before I marry him. Papa, his judgment so good about people. I'd like to marry a man Papa thought well of. It make all the difference in the way the children treat him. But now. Well, now I'll have to write him and tell him not to come. I can't let him waste his furlough. I . . . I won't be any good and I wouldn't want to marry him and not to make him happy. I'd rather he marry somebody else who could make him happy."

"I know what's worrying you, Serena," I said. "Really. I

88

thought it would be and I didn't know how to bring the subject up. You haven't written that letter yet, have you?"

"No," she said, "but it gotta be done tonight or tomorrow at the latest. I put it off as long as I could."

"Well, thank God for that," I said, "because you're wrong about this. You really are mistaken."

And not to fail now, that was the thing. To choose the words carefully so that clarity would be accomplished without shocking. But what her words *were*, I didn't know. If a uterus was a womb, what did she call . . . ? But to be convincing, is it really so much a matter of words or of manner, after all? I sat back in my chair and lit a cigarette. "You be patient with me a little while," I said, "and pretty soon you're going to feel a lot better about things. I just have to think the right way to say this."

She smiled at me a little timidly. "Look," I said. "That day you got back from the clinic, I heard Fedora and that other woman talking about 'bedroom furniture.' I know they got to you. I wanted to spare you that, and I got here too late. But if they hadn't, others would have. A time like this, you remember every stray word you ever heard in your life."

"That true," she said, "the oddest things come back, things I heard Miss Addie speak of, old things . . ."

"And it's all spoken in ignorance, Serena. In superstition, that's the trouble. They don't know what they're talking about. Your worry is, you're going to cheat Mr. Devereaux. Isn't that so?"

"That right," she said.

"Well, you won't be able to have children," I said, "so **you** will have to tell him that to be honest with him. Did he count a lot on children, do you think?"

"No," she said. "We talked about that. He not so crazy for children, like some people. But he want to be *loved*."

"Well, if it's all right with him about the children, then **you** won't have cheated him, because that is the *only* thing that will be different, except that you'll be well and you'll be happier and make a better wife not being sick."

I don't know as I ever had such attention, or such politeness, either, but one thing I didn't have, and that was belief. "Your nervous system will be the same," I said. "It isn't going to change. There aren't any nerves in the womb. You didn't feel that tumor while it was growing, now, did you? Think how if it had been on your arm or your face."

I put out my cigarette and resisted an immediate desire to light a fresh one, thinking how unconvincing that would appear. "All your personal relations" (personal relations? where had I got that term?) "will be the same," I said. "What I mean is, you'll make love just the same, the very same, as you do now. Nothing about that will be changed. The womb doesn't have anything to do with making love, Serena. It's for holding babies."

Well, now, there was something different on her face, quite remarkably like hope. "Look," I said, "if you want, I could draw you a picture of it."

For weeks I had not seen her move so quickly. She went into the kitchen and came back with a pencil, a knife and paper. She turned to sharpen the pencil so that the shavings would fall into the wood box. "Oh, that would be so nice," she said. "I would like to know. I would like so much to know."

And I was really very well equipped, one way or another, to handle this drawing, as though I had been carefully preparing myself for this very day, even as a child. In the museum, while the other kids had cared for nothing but dinosaurs, there I had been glued to the muscle man and the glass fellow with his colored tubes inside and the transparent lady. Even the little embryos in their glass bottles, I knew them all by heart long before the science courses, the courses in hygiene and anatomy. Who cared now that I never knew a brontosaurus from a stego-saurus? I moved my chair around beside Serena's so we could share the drawing. "Well, here's the womb," I said. "It's not

90

nearly so large as women imagine it. Of course, with a baby or a tumor in it, that's different, but normally it's about like your fist and the importance women give to it, you'd think it filled half the body. Then, the ligaments. They're sort of like that lamp cord, there, and they're attached here and here and here. And here are the tubes, like this, and then the ovaries. They're not much bigger than an almond."

"Is that *true?*" she said.

"None of it," I said, "is so big as women make out in their minds. O.K., so here's the womb like this. I think it would be easier to see from the side. I'll start over. Yes, now that's better. Well, here's the womb and here's the canal and here's the vagina. The bladder's in front of the womb and the rectum's behind it."

Serena studied the drawing with careful attention, as though her life depended on it. "The surgeon," I said, "is probably going to cut somewhere along here." I drew a horizontal line clear across the drawing at the lower level of the uterus. "Now," I said, "everything below that line is going to be the same as it is right now. The vagina's there, the canal's there, your nervous system's the same, the way you feel, the way you make love, everything's going to be left just the way it was."

She kept studying the drawing as though if she looked away it might disappear. Suddenly I lost all faith in drawings, diagrams, explanations. I put my hand over the drawing so she would look at me. "I give you my word," I said. "It's honest for you to marry Mr. Devereaux if you tell him you can't have children."

Serena's eyes suddenly filled with tears. "Oh," she said. "Oh, I thank you so. You've taken such a load off my mind." She put her arms around me in sudden exuberance and then she sat back and looked at me. "Just imagine," she said, "you comin here on just the right day and knowin just the right thing to say. Often people come to see you at the right time, but they say the wrong thing. Or if they say the right thing, it's too late, too late."

"Well," I said, "show me the pictures now."

Albert Devereaux was extraordinarily handsome. He was tall

and very slender and he had a neat mustache. He seemed a more sophisticated, more complicated person than Mrs. Covington and I hoped he knew the value of what he was getting, he who "wanted to be loved."

"He's very good looking," I said, "and what's more, he looks like the kind of man who'd like to decide for himself whether to get married or not."

"And have time to do it in, too," Serena said. "My, I hope he can get that furlough postponed. It would be so awful for me to be in the hospital all the time he had off."

"We need the time," I said. "It's going to take you several weeks after you get out of the hospital before you're really feeling good, you know, and I'll bet you haven't got a thing ready for your trousseau."

"I'll show you something," she said, "you won't think me too foolish." She went into the closet then and came back with a long, flat department-store box. Inside, carefully wrapped in tissue paper, was a beautiful white satin nightgown.

"Ah, that's the way," I said. "First things first." And the two of us started laughing to be so sweetly let down from the tense and emotional afternoon. "You'll look beautiful in it," I said, "and you'll be happy in it, too. I'd better go now so you can get that letter written. You going to invite us to the wedding?"

"I dearly love to have you," she said. "Would you come?"

I wonder if we'll be here by then, I thought, but a note of sadness was not what we needed then. As I walked home, still filled with happiness, I thought of the days and days before when I had left this house feeling so frustrated and impotent against the secret of her sadness. It was, as she had said about Joey's wanting to be an electrician, so very true: everybody like to be a success.

"Well, *well*," Ted said, when he saw me. "What happened to you?"

"Today," I said, "I did something right for a change."

"I don't know if I did or not," he said. "I invited Major Miller and his family out for a picnic in the woods this Sunday."

"Fine," I said. "It'll be fun. We'll have a big fire and cook outdoors."

"Well," Ted said, "you know they're such great campers and all that, and all through these rains they've been shut up in that apartment in the city and the kids are wild to get out."

I could believe it. The Millers had three boys, nine, seven and five, and they were very active. Suddenly I had a vision of the car stopping in front, the three boys bursting out of it, bursting into the house and, after that long drive, bursting straight into the bathroom where, naturally, they all grabbed that rotten rag of Wilkies' towel, from which they immediately developed pink-eye, ringworm, impetigo. . . .

8

ON SUNDAY the Millers drove slowly by the house and Ted
started out to meet them, for there were no house numbers and
the streets didn't even have names. On a sudden impulse I picked
up Wilkie's towel with a Kleenex, put it in a paper bag by his
door and put up fresh towels before going out to greet the
Millers. We all started for the woods immediately and on the
path I signaled Ted to hang back for a moment. "I've done it,"
I said. "You'll have to stand by me now when we get home."

"Done what?"

"I threw out Wilkie's towel and put fresh ones up."

"Oh oh," he said.

After the picnic we saw the Millers off and then went like
condemned people up the front steps. There was a light on in
Wilkie's place. The paper sack had disappeared and the new
towel had been used. Ted and I went into our kitchen to make
coffee and await the explosion. Nothing happened. We had a
light supper and did the dishes and still nothing had happened.

94

"I can't stand the suspense," I said. "Go invite him in for a cup of coffee and let's get this over with."

Ted walked into our living room, opened the door to the hall, closed it and came right back to the kitchen.

"What's the matter?" I said.

"His door's open," he said, "and he's sitting in the center of the room on a box reading a comic book."

"Well?"

"That's all," Ted said. "That box, that's all there is in the room. The place is absolutely bare."

"Maybe he'd even *like* a cup of coffee," I said. "Ask him, will you?"

Oh, he would, he would. He jumped up as soon as he understood and came in behind Ted. "Evenin, Mrs. Demerest," he said. "Very nice of yall to ask me in."

So I poured the coffee, meanwhile deciding that, about the towel, I would be folksy and neighborly, something like *I thought while I was picking up after two I might as well pick up after three.*

"Wheah does it all go?" Wilkie said. "Ah don know. Ah bought four complete houses of furniture and there ain't nothin but one bed left of it. Wheah does it all go? Ah caint figure it. Ah moved on four jobs in three years; I guess it gits lost. Busted maybe. I dunno."

So Ted asked him about his present job and he described every small action of the entire routine of his work (and yes, he did carry a gun around the prisoners and yes, he was very afraid of them) and he talked until the coffee was gone. We silently gave up our plans for the evening and I got out some cake and made some tea to go with it. Mr. Wilkie liked tea, too, and especially he liked cake, and he talked steadily to the end of both. Now we were on the Navy and on how, always, all his life, he had wanted to be in the Navy. He got a high-school education for no other reason than to get into the Navy and then he had to have his parents' consent. Well, he worked on his father for a solid six months and he finally got his consent. Then he had to win over his mother.

Marveling at Mr. Wilkie's bladder I now made some cocoa, since we were out of everything else. He liked cocoa very much, too, and he told us all the horrors, the anxieties, of winning over his mother. It was by now 11:30 and Ted's eyes were drooping so I mentioned how he had to get up early in the morning. Wilkie agreed that yes, they did have to get up early in the morning and he certainly did appreciate the Lieutenant waking him up every morning.

Finally, he said, he *did* win over his mother, with only an extra year wasted in addition to all that time in high school, and he dashed down to the Navy to enlist and that was where he found out he had flat feet. They wouldn't take him. He never had found anything he liked since. That was the onliest thing he had ever wanted and he had tried everything to unflatten his feet, but nothin was any good. "Nothin evah hurt me so bad as that," he said. "Not havin my wife leave me. Nor losin ma children. Nothin."

He saw that the cocoa was all gone and if he had eyes in his head he saw that Ted was all but asleep, too. "Well, Ah certainly thank you for the coffee," he said. "It's been a real pleasure." And he got up to leave. He had talked for over four solid hours and he hadn't once mentioned the towel.

Every day I gave him a clean bath towel and wash cloth, which he used. In a couple of days a supply of strongly scented hand soap called "Wanda" showed up in the bathroom. A few days later several rolls of toilet paper appeared on the shelf. I considered the matter agreeably settled and did not discount how difficult it must be for a man who carried such disappointment to make any gesture at all.

The Americans had landed in French Africa in early November and, as though to express the encouragement that everybody felt at this, the weather suddenly turned mild and warm, like spring. The creek was clear of mud again, sparkling as we had

96

first seen it. Every time Ted was home in daylight we would get a rowboat and go out on the creek. Now and then we would pass a solitary fisherman sitting on the bank. Another time we saw a ladder held against the bank by vines which had grown around it. At the top of the ladder there was a small clearing in the center of which was a tiny cabin. It seemed deserted and the ladder beckoned with such invitation we could not resist it. We pulled the boat over to the bank, tied it, climbed the ladder and found ourselves in a space completely roofed over with trees. There were no signs of life. The cabin seemed enchanted, hidden there in this great quiet, so secret. The door was unlocked. Inside there was a fireplace and on either side of it a bed. On one bed was a blue nightgown. On the other a pair of striped pajamas. Between the beds sat a great jug of whisky, about a third full.

You could easily see how it had all happened. They had lain there, she in her blue nightgown, he in his striped pajamas, passing the jug back and forth until at last they had simply floated out of their clothing and away, possibly up the chimney.

Day after day the springlike weather held, and it would all have been perfect except that Mrs. Covington had gone to the hospital and been turned away because there was no room in the colored ward. Another five dollars had been shot to hell, more time accumulated when she was unable to work, and the first payment was due at the bank before she had even got started on the operation she was paying for. Fortunately she had, to sustain her, frequent letters from Mr. Devereaux, who had successfully postponed his furlough and would now wait until she was out of the hospital and over her operation.

"If only we could have weather like this when you are able to go to the woods with me," I said. "There are so many plants I don't know and so many things you must show me and now it is just heavenly. By the time you get out of the hospital it will be snowing, I suppose, or raining again."

"I do wish I could get it over with," she said. "I can't work like this and I have to get back to work. Christmas is going to be here and I must get some money saved by Christmas for the children's presents."

"What do they want for Christmas?"

"They say they don't want nothin. They know that I borrowed money from the bank and they won't tell me what they want. They need clothes, though. They both of them outgrown everything."

"Do you think it would help any if I talked to anybody at the hospital?"

"No," she said, "the colored ward is full. I saw it. There's nothin to do but wait."

"Today in the woods," I said, "I saw something I'd never seen before, a little dark green plant with thick leaves, growing flat on the ground. I reached down to pick a piece of it and it came right up with me, only it was still attached to the ground, and when I pulled I thought the whole floor of the woods was coming up. There wasn't any end to it."

"That sound like runnin pine," she said, "or else runnin cedar. Did you bring some with you?"

"No," I said. "It's too tough. I couldn't break it."

"Well, there's two kinds," she said, "and that surely what it was. One looks exactly like a pine branch and the other like cedar, but they grow flat on the ground under the oak leaves. When you see a piece you pick it up and go like you gone walk away, and then you see it all come up behind you. It's hard to find, though, I'll admit. It never grow on a path. You got to be walkin over leaves and scuffin them."

"When you're well, will you go to the woods with me?" I said. "There must be so many things you could show me about them that I miss."

"Ah," she said, "I like to go to the woods with you. I wish . . . Oh, but I couldn't make it over rough ground now, I know."

"Oh, no," I said. "We'll wait till you're well."

98

"But that will be after Christmas," she said, "and I was thinkin how nice it be . . ."

"Whenever we get to do it," I said, "it's going to be nice."

"I remember," she said, "before Christmas we all used to go to the woods for runnin pine and runnin cedar and for moss to put under the tree. Of course Papa used to go hisself to get the tree and he always bring back wintergreen leaves for us to chew. But we would go in a big group to get the runnin pine and runnin cedar. These, with hemlock, we would put all around the door frames and window frames and around the pictures. Holly, too, with the red berries, we would get. I remember once (this was when we were bigger) there were a lot of us ready to go and John, my brother, he had his gun. 'Leave your gun,' we said to him. 'It just be in the way.' But John said he knew something we didn't know and he kept his gun. Sure enough, when we got to the woods there was mistletoe and John said, 'I don't know why it is mistletoe always grow too high to reach.' And so he shot it down, a big clump of it, and we all divide it up."

"I'll bring you some running pine," I said. "That is, if I can find the place again."

"Oh, Joey know lots of places," she said. "If you can't find it again, I sure he can find some. There used to be a lot over by Dead Man Hill, but that's a long way."

"I never heard of it," I said. "Which direction is it?"

"Oh, my," she said, "I don't know if I could describe how to get there or not. It so hard to find. You know," she said, looking up at me suddenly, "if you promise not to laugh, I'll tell you a story."

"I promise."

"You won't laugh," she said, "but you won't believe, either. Well, anyhow, there's supposed to be a place near Dead Man Hill . . . Now you won't laugh?"

I shook my head.

"Well, once when we were children, we were comin down Dead Man Hill and some men on horses came behind us, ridin

99

and chasin us to frighten us. I don't know what we stumble on maybe, but they didn't want us there. We children all very scared and we ran for the woods to hide from the men and suddenly we came to a place, I don't know how to say. Somethin seem to come over us and we feel our hair stand on end."

This must have been where she feared I would laugh, because she looked at me questioningly before she went on. "Our grandmother was here then and we ran home as fast as we could and told her. Grandmother said she knew well the place we meant, that she, too, had come on it once and had her hair stand on end. Another time, later, we all huntin runnin pine and runnin cedar and we got lost. We look around and there we were in the same place and . . ."

"And did your hair stand on end again?"

"Yes," she said, "it did. There's a story that there's buried treasure there. Some say the body of a murdered man is buried there. I never found anybody said they knew."

"I want to go there," I said, "but if it's so far, we won't do that first. We'll take some very little walks together first and see how you do. We'd better work up to Dead Man Hill gradually. Maybe we'll take a lunch first time so we'll be sure to sit and rest awhile."

She was sitting in her little rocker and she looked at me with a curious expression on her face. "I'm gone get well," she said, "if for no other reason than to go to the woods with you. I'm gone do that. I'm gone walk in the woods with you." She spoke with such unaccustomed defiance that suddenly I doubted if she were as confident about the operation as I had thought. "Why, Mrs. Covington," I said, "you aren't in doubt that you will get well, are you?"

"Why, no," she said. "Of course not."

The next morning Redley Stuart staggered up the back stair with a hundred pounds of ice on his back. He managed, quite purple in the face, to get it into the box and then he more or less felt where the kitchen chair was and sank into it. His sad-eyed hound leaned against his legs, sat, and sighed as Stuart sighed.

"You look all in," I said. "You'd better have a cup of coffee. Where's Benedict?"

"Oh, Benedict," Redley said. "He's in jail." He took out a handkerchief and wiped his forehead. "I will take that coffee, please, ma'am," he said.

"In jail? What for?"

"Oh, stealin a watch," he said, taking the cup from me. "At least, that's the charge."

"Well, I . . . I find that hard to believe about Benedict," I said. "Do *you* believe it?"

Redley moved his chair so that he could set the cup on the table. His hand was shaking from the unaccustomed exertion. "Of course I don't believe it," he said. "Why, Benedict worked for me for years. Land, I couldn't have a thief on that wagon. Benedict has to go into places where they got two, three hundred dollars' worth of liquor sitting around, bars, restaurants. . . ."

"And he never takes any of the liquor, does he?"

"Of course not," Redley said. "Why, I'd send Benedict into any place."

"Benedict didn't say he *did* take the watch, did he?"

"Of course not," Redley said, patiently.

"Well, who did?"

"Why, that . . . that fellah they always have do it. This guy he goes around till he finds some nigra in the pool hall alone, and he drops this same old watch in his pocket and then he goes for a policeman. Then of course he's got witnesses and Benedict hasn't got a witness, so the judge says *two weeks*. I talked to the judge already. 'In two weeks my back's going to be broken, Judge,' I said to him. Honestly, I couldn't get comfortable last night. I must have tried a thousand positions."

I sat down at the kitchen table. The old hound looked up at me and nodded. "But Mr. Stuart," I said, "I don't understand.

What's the point of it? This fellow, whoever he is, what's he got against Benedict? What does he gain by it?"

"He's got nothing against Benedict," he said, "in particular. He's just doing what he's told. They just got to get enough big strong guys in there to fix these roads. You know before the rains they were bad enough, but since the flood, why, they're terrible, Mrs. Demerest. I don't remember I ever saw the roads in such a condition."

"You mean they always repair the roads with prison labor?"

"Why, of course," Redley said. "That's mighty good coffee, Mrs. Demerest. Could I trouble you?"

"Certainly, Mr. Stuart. But, tell me, what are you going to do about Benedict?"

"Do? I've already done everything I can. I've talked to Judge Rollins, and I didn't get anywhere. I *told* him how bad I need Benedict. I told him I'd pay a fine, anything. But he just said to me, 'Redley, you'll live. I need that nigger worse than you do.'"

"But aren't you going to get him a lawyer?"

"A lawyer? My land, Mrs. Demerest, now where you think I'm going to find a lawyer to take a nigra case?"

"Well, there certainly are lawyers who defend colored clients," I said.

"Oh, Up Nawth," he said. "I suppose so. But my goodness, Benedict's sentence is only two weeks."

There were so many things to jump at all at once, and I realized I was losing my temper. It wouldn't do Benedict any good to convince Stuart that I was sure the Nawth didn't have any corner on attorneys who defended colored clients. "Two weeks haven't got anything to do with it," I said. "If he isn't guilty, it's the same as two minutes or two years. The idea of ruining a man's good name in order to . . ."

"Now, Mrs. Demerest," Stuart said. "I'm very sorry I got you all worried and upset with my troubles."

"*Your* troubles?" I was ready to scream at him.

"You're always so pleasant," he said. "It's such a pleasure to come here. Benedict, he fairly worships you, you know. Benedict, why he'd just never forgive me if he thought I had you all worried and upset over this with my fool complainin."

"Oh, Mr. Stuart," I said, "will you quit throwing your charm around all over my kitchen? You know perfectly well I'm not worried and upset, as you call it. I'm sore. I think this is the most outrageous . . ."

"Now, Mrs. Demerest," he said, "we got to be broadminded about this."

"Broadminded?"

"Yes," he said, in his pleasant, soft voice. "We've got to look at it from the judge's point of view. You know, Mrs. Demerest, those roads really are in a deplorable condition."

9

"HOW ARE YOU feeling today?" I said to Mrs. Covington.

"About the same," she said.

"I'm glad you're not worse," I said, sitting down by the chair where she sat mending clothes, "because I need so very much to talk to you."

"Why, what is it?" she said.

"Well, you remember that time I got so angry at Taylor Frye about the five dollars he charges you," I said, "and how it upset you so? I want very much to be sure I don't do it again and I've been waiting at home two hours, so I'd be sure to be calm. As a matter of fact, I wasn't going to talk to you at all, but to Mr. Loftis, only the store is full of people and I can't. It's about Benedict who works on the ice truck for Mr. Stuart."

"Oh, yes," she said.

"You knew he was in jail?"

"I heard," she said.

"Well, Redley Stuart and I had a conversation that was straight out of *Alice in Wonderland*. It didn't meet anyplace.

It seems to me that Benedict ought to have a lawyer. Or, at least, he ought to have the opportunity to have a lawyer."

She had stopped her mending and she looked at me now, very attentively.

"Oh, you don't need to act with me as though you're walking on eggs," I said. "I learned my lesson. In any case, I wouldn't *do* anything without Ted."

She quite visibly relaxed at this. "The Captain," she said, "he surely will tell you how different it is here from Up North."

"Oh, yes," I said, "he's very aware of the difference, especially how possible it is in the North to talk all your life and never to be faced with the need to act. You've lived in the North," I said, "and you know there are people who can *talk* a fine liberal line while they're signing a restrictive real estate covenant. In fact, you know perfectly well that the North isn't any paradise at all. It's cold, it's expensive, the slums are worse—in short there's only one thing that could possibly make it worth a colored person's effort to go there."

"Education," she said. "Yes, it's so. But still, about Benedict . . ."

"Well, about Benedict," I said. "I think whether Ted agrees with me or not, he'd like to have some information from somebody besides Redley Stuart, and that's what I've come for."

"What did Mr. Stuart say?"

"It's so weird, I don't know if I can tell you," I said, "but I'll try." So I reported to her as best I could the conversation, but the non sequiturs that in the last two hours had become almost funny to me caused not a single smile on her face.

"Well, yes, that's about the way I think it seem to Mr. Stuart," she said. "You know, Mrs. Demerest, Benedict he very fond of Mr. Stuart. He very likely be satisfied that Mr. Stuart tried."

"I get the feeling I'm shouting into a deaf world," I said, "but maybe it's just as important that *I'm* not satisfied. Maybe it's more important that they shouldn't think they could go framing people by dropping watches in their pockets and not have somebody *notice*. Oh, wait a minute. You don't think, yourself, that Benedict stole a watch, do you?"

"Oh, no," she said, "but Benedict, he don't even a little bit think Mr. Stuart believe that, either."

"Well," I said, "I know that Redley Stuart is wrong about no lawyer would defend a colored man. I know there are lawyers who do."

"Mrs. Demerest," she said, in her quiet way, "you don't have in your mind, do you, something like callin in the N.A.A.C.P. or anything like that?"

"Oh, no," I said. "Give me credit for some sense of proportion. I'm not trying to make a Scottsboro case out of a charge of petty theft. I don't want to make Benedict out a martyr. I just want him to have the simplest thing that's due him whether he did or did not steal a watch. And if Ted thinks so, too, and if we find an attorney and the attorney goes to the jail and talks to Benedict, what's the harm?"

Mrs. Covington got up slowly out of her chair. "I so like to do something to make you feel a little better," she said, "and I can't think what to say. I put on the kettle."

I moved out to the kitchen with her. "You don't have any information, then, that you think Ted ought to know, that's very different from Redley Stuart's?"

She was measuring tea into the pot and she waited until she had finished counting and put the lid back tight on the canister. "Well, there is something I like to say," she said. "I don't know if you call it information or not."

"Well?"

She sat down on one of the kitchen chairs across the table from me. "It seem like," she said, "I'm always talking about money to you. I hate for you to think I care about nothing but money."

"I don't," I said. "How could I? Besides, if we're talking about lawyers it's certainly something that has to be considered."

"That just it," she said. "Now Mr. Stuart is right about any lawyer near here. There isn't one in Chinkapink."

106

"It must be Taylor Frye never thought of it yet," I said, "but he will, in time."

She smiled to herself and lowered her eyes. Even with me she couldn't *join* in a joke about Taylor Frye. "But," she went on, "I expect if you were to go into Lawtonville you might could find one. You could, I'm sure, if it was a murder or something like that. But if you could, Mrs. Demerest, don't you realize what it *cost* to get a lawyer to come that distance?"

"I know," I said, "that's one reason I wouldn't do anything without talking to Ted first. I suppose it might be a hundred, hundred and fifty dollars before the thing was done with."

"Yes!" she said.

"But of course a reputable lawyer would go into that with us first, so that at least we could find out if it were possible to try at all or not."

"But," she said, rather impatiently, and then stopped herself. She poured the tea wordlessly, unconsciously holding her side in the gesture which had by now become habitual with her. She smiled at me and said, "Mrs. Demerest, maybe it wouldn't be your choice. It wouldn't be the Captain's choice. I don't even think . . . No, I don't think it would be Papa's choice, but I can practically guarantee to you that Benedict would rather work for two weeks on the roads than pay out a hundred dollars he hasn't got."

"Oh, Lord," I said, "you didn't think what I had in mind was to get Benedict saddled with a big debt?"

"Well, who would pay, then?" she said.

"Why, we would," I said. "I supposed you took it for granted that if we messed into things, we'd naturally take the responsibility. It's one of the reasons I'm having to go so carefully. If we had hundreds of dollars to throw around, I'd have *done* something by now."

"But why you think Benedict wouldn't rather work on the roads than to owe you and the Captain a hundred dollars?"

"But he *wouldn't* owe us," I said. "It wouldn't be his doing; it would be ours."

"Now, if Benedict got you a lawyer, wouldn't you think you owe Benedict the money?"

"Well, yes," I said, "I would."

"Why you think Benedict be any different, then?"

"Oh," I said. "Well, you made your point. And it's a good one, too. I suppose I sounded patronizing to think somehow we . . ."

"Oh, now," she said, "now Mrs. Demerest, I know you meant the best. I know you not like those people that only talk for the colored."

"Well, all right," I said, "you gave me a different picture from Redley Stuart's, and that's what I came for. I do see now that Benedict might choose to do this in his own way rather than have somebody pay for him."

"I glad," she said. "I very glad you taking it in the way I meant. I feel very bad if your feelings are hurt."

"Only," I said, "I still think that Benedict himself ought to have the choice. Even if he wants to turn it down, I think he should have that much right, anyhow."

This disappointed her, I saw, for she had apparently felt that the matter was settled. "You said you wanted to talk to Papa about it," she said, "but the store too full."

"Well, yes, I was afraid really of getting you upset."

"How would this be?" she said. "Suppose I talk to Papa about it over here and I let you know what Papa think."

"Well, yes," I said. "Ted would like to know that, I'm sure. That's a good idea. I wouldn't be surprised if Ted would maybe be satisfied to go by Mr. Loftis' advice."

"That's what we'll do, then," she said. "I'll talk to Papa sometime today, I promise you, and I'll send one of the children down when they get home from school to tell you if Papa like you to come up, or what."

Ted got home early that night, for which I was very glad.

He had a quick snack to stave off his hunger so I could post-pone getting dinner until he'd heard about my talk with Redley Stuart. I had barely finished reporting on my visit with Mrs. Covington when Sarah came to the back door.

"Come in, Sarah," I said.

"I brought you this letter from my grandfather," she said. "It's for you and the Captain."

"Sarah," Ted said, "what do you think? If I ever do get to be a captain, what will your grandfather call me then?"

Sarah laughed slyly behind her hand. "Oh, Captain Demerest," she said, "you know he'll call you Major, then."

"That's what I thought," Ted said.

"Grandpa he says if you call a man Captain, he feel like a captain and pretty soon he'll be a captain."

"Only some men, Sarah. You know, some lieutenants, if you call them Captain, all they feel is inadequate."

"I got to go," Sarah said. "Grandpa want me to come right back. Oh, Mrs. Demerest, I forgot to tell you. Mamma said to tell you she called the hospital and they going to take her in tomorrow."

"Oh, Sarah, I'm so glad. Can I help her any?"

"No, ma'am. She got everything all ready."

And so we read Mr. Loftis' letter.

Dear Captain Demerest and Mrs. Demerest,

I tell this letter to my granddaughter, Sarah, so be sure she write down everything exactly as I say it to you. Sarah she always very careful about her writing, you know. Now, about Benedict Wilson, I naturally pleased that you honor my advice. I want you to know that I know you both concerned with the rights of this thing and I am going to see that Benedict knows what you stood ready for.

But I advise you wait till Benedict's sentence over, just quietly. I hope you believe me that this might do Benedict good.

Captain Demerest, Mrs. Demerest, Benedict's name among the colored is not thief. His name is foolish. Any colored as old as Benedict should know not to go in that pool hall after the rains come.

Yours respectfully,

ABEL LOFTIS

Well, now we had the word from Mr. Loftis. I got up to start dinner. "Honestly," I said. "They talk about roads, about money, about 'foolish.' It just seems impossible to have a simple exchange of conversation about a man's rights."

Ted shook his head. "We know what Redley Stuart thinks," he said, "and we know what Mrs. Covington thinks and now we know what Mr. Loftis thinks. Nobody seems to care what Benedict thinks."

"I'd like to know," I said.

"So would I," Ted said. "You'd think I could just go over to the jail and ask him, but I don't know. . . . In a state where they make *judges* responsible for the condition of the roads . . . Tell you what," he said. "I think I'll walk over and talk to Clarence Rochelle. We've been riding together quite a while now, and it's *his* car."

"We've got so many opinions," I said. "We might as well have one more."

When Ted got home, dinner was ready, so I let him have a start on it before I pressed for the news. "We have a different opinion, all right," he said. "You'd have to be absolutely humorless to try to make a civil rights case out of this thing by now. You know what Clarence told me? He said that Benedict has always been pretty proud of his strength and that in a way he probably took it as a compliment, because they only go after the real strong guys."

"A *compliment?*"

"Well, Clarence said this has been going on a long time and there's a sort of rivalry among the ones who get arrested to see

110

who's the strongest on the roads. The girls come out to watch them if the weather's nice."

"It's crazy," I said. "The whole thing. Why, this morning it was a matter of whether a man had a right to a lawyer or not and by nightfall it's a Dostoyevsky novel."

"You see what people miss who have electric refrigerators," Ted said.

"But Ted. . ."

"Yes?"

"Well, where does that leave *us?*"

"I'm damned if I know," he said. "But what Clarence suggests is that I buy a carton of cigarettes for Benedict, which Clarence says *he* should take to the jail, and to make *me* feel better, he'll ask Benedict whether he wants a lawyer or not. And that's what I'm going to do."

The next night Ted came home on the bus and walked the two miles from Hester so that Clarence could go to the jail alone, as he seemed to prefer. He had promised to come over that evening and report. He came, as all of them except Joey now came, to the back door.

"Sit down, Clarence," I said.

"Oh, no, thank you, ma'am," he said, holding his hat before him. "I got to get along home right away. I just stopped by to tell you all about Benedict."

"You saw him, then?" Ted said.

"Yes, sir," Clarence said. "I surely did."

"Well, what did he say?" Ted said.

"Aw, you know how Benedict is," Clarence said, "or I guess Mrs. Demerest does, anyways. You know, Benedict he never say much."

"I know," I said.

"Well, I told him what . . . what we talked about, you know, what you say, Lieutenant, but he just smile and shake his head. I guess he don't want no lawyer. His time, it's only got ten days to go."

"He didn't say anything, then?" Ted said.

"Well, yes. Yes, he did, Lieutenant. He said, 'Clarence, you be sure to thank the Captain for the cigarettes.'"

"Oh," Ted said. "Well, thank you very much for going to all the trouble, Clarence. I know it made you late and all."

"I'll be gettin on home, then," Clarence said. "I see you in the mornin same time, Lieutenant?"

"Clarence," I said, for suddenly like a rejected child I wanted terribly to salvage something out of this mad, frustrating day, "didn't Benedict have any message for me, anything at all?"

Clarence, at the door, stopped and looked down at his feet. He was smiling. "Well, yes, Mrs. Demerest, yes he did, but I don't know if you gone like it or not."

"Oh, that's all right," I said. "Tell me. What did he say?"

"Benedict say," he said, and he looked at me sideways, still smiling. "He say, 'And tell Mrs. Demerest not to forget to empty the pan under the icebox.'"

10

THE SPARKLING weather held on into the last days of November, and each day as I stepped out into it and tasted it with such pleasure I thought surely there could only be one person who could be savoring it more, and that would be Judge Rollins, as he thought of how greatly it facilitated the repair of the county roads.

The book I was then working on had, along with our household, miraculously settled into a flowing order so that it seemed effortlessly to move of itself. These days I carried it with me into the woods when I gathered fagots. I had found a lovely hollowed-out place, bedded with thick moss, where I often wrote. When I would stop and look up, there was now the most perfect thing to contemplate. Directly ahead was a small, solitary persimmon tree from which all the leaves had fallen, allowing each of the fruits to show golden and light-catching, dangling from its single stem. If I lay back, my head pillowed on my arms, these hanging golden teardrops would be etched against clear blue sky, with sometimes a fluid white cloud caught in perfect balance a little to the right and above the tree. Out of sight, but still audible, was the creek. Seen from this angle, so that the thick, spongy oak-leaf, moss and vine world of the ground could be discounted, the little scene had a Chinese quality, an austerity that quite transported me and speeded the transition from domestic urgencies to that necessarily timeless place where one writes. Very often the golden persimmons would seem to swell and fade as though they breathed, and I would fall asleep to dream whole sequences of the book to come.

The beautiful weather even brought out Mrs. Emerson, though she seemed not to be aware of the weather, for she was dressed exactly as she had been for the rain in the old collarless brown coat fastened with the safety pin, the same old rag tied over her head. I had gone, as I did every day now, to Mr. Loftis' store to hear if there was word from the hospital. Two days before there had been the news that the operation was over and that Serena had survived it. The store was rather crowded, and I was only waiting until Mr. Loftis should have a moment, when suddenly I saw him move out from behind the counter and run, heavy as he was, toward the door.

"Why, Mrs. Emerson," he said, "how very, very nice to see you this fine day. You just come right on in. Now you wait there a moment till I get you something fix to sit on."

Never had I seen him move so fast, though his movements were always surprisingly light for his size. He ran into the back room and returned with one of the beautiful sacks like the one I used for gathering fagots. This he spread over an upturned box. "There now," he said. "Now it's nice and clean for you, Mrs. Emerson." It was not that he pulled or lifted her, exactly; it was just that he seemed to be all around her, hovering and supporting until, by a zigzag kind of progress, she had actually done what he wanted. And then, once she was down and, without falling, had seated herself, she sighed with great weariness and looking up at him she smiled weakly. "Oh, thank you," she said. "Yes, I'll rest awhile, Abel."

114

"Wouldn't you like some ice cream?" he said. "Or perhaps a cool drink. It's very warm for November, this year."

"Why, thank you," she said. "Yes, I would like some ice cream."

"Yes, yes," he said. "Just a minute. I run over and get you a clean spoon."

"I'll go, Abel," a colored woman said, and ran out the door. As though this sign of life had somehow galvanized the whole store, the other customers shook themselves from their intense watching of the little scene, and one by one they began to go up to the mad, filthy old woman as though she were some kind of queen. "Evenin, Mrs. Emerson." "How yall, Mrs. Emerson?" "I so glad to see you, Mrs. Emerson." It was like the low murmur of the devout and Mrs. Emerson sat there nodding her head to each one, saying, "Hello, dear. Thank you, dear," and (to the woman who came back with a spoon and a large table napkin) "That's sweet of you, dear." Mr. Loftis came now with the container of ice cream and he took the napkin from the woman and spread it out in all its shining whiteness over the spotted filth of that brown-coated lap, and he held the spoon near Mrs. Emerson's warped claw until she had managed to grasp it, all, all with such exquisite tenderness as one cares for a dear sick baby.

The shock of the contrast with essentially this same scene in the white grocery beat upon me so that I had the feeling I must stay perfectly still and not mar the ritual, as though somehow I had got into the wrong church by mistake, a church where everyone else knew perfectly the esoteric rites that I might disturb. All the other customers happened to be colored and I moved back quietly into the shadows and waited but I saw that I waited no more patiently than the others. They seemed content that no orders would be taken, no business conducted, until Mrs. Emerson should have been settled and announced herself quite satisfied, as presently she did, with the flavor of the ice cream.

"That's good," Mr. Loftis said. "I very glad you like it. You just sit there now and enjoy it, Mrs. Emerson. You rest awhile. I take care of my customers and then I'll come back to see if there something else I can do for you. We always very honored, very honored, to have you come here." And he *backed* away from her, exactly as if she had been a queen, and this seemed to be the signal that whoever among the customers had children with them would take the children by the hand and lead them up to Mrs. Emerson so that they—visibly awed and impressed— might curtsy before her. It seemed to me that it would be perfectly fitting if the strange creature should reach out with her gnarled, misshapen claw and anoint them with a spoon of ice cream.

But she only acknowledged each child's presence with a little nod of her head and went on eating her ice cream with as much delicacy as the condition of her hands allowed. I remembered how obstreperously she had eaten ice cream in Roebuck's Grocery, how she had stuck out her tongue and licked the wooden spoon, and I was sure now (as I had suspected then) that she had deliberately acted in a way to infuriate and defy the people in the store. Somehow I forgot her ugliness and her dirt. In the dim afternoon light of the store, and at this distance, she seemed slowly to become the very essence of what they made her out to be.

Mr. Loftis began to take care of his customers, very efficiently, like a man who had everything under control, who was watching over everything, until suddenly he noticed me, with a widening of his eyes, and it was clear that he had forgotten about me. "Oh, I didn't want anything," I said. "I only stopped by to see if you had news of Mrs. Covington today."

"They say she doing nicely," he said. "I called the hospital about noon. And I thank you for your interest, Mrs. Demerest. I do indeed." He grabbed up one of the charge pads from a pigeon-hole and went up to Mrs. Emerson, then. "And now," he said to her, "what you like to order, Mrs. Emerson? Anything at all you need, I write it down here on the charge pad. You know your credit always good here."

Mrs. Emerson began to order groceries which, he assured her, would be delivered, and as I left the store I saw that he was only pretending to write on the pad and would repeat after her, carefully, each item.

"Oh, it is so discouraging," I said to Ted later when I had reported this still further mystery about Mrs. Emerson, "to find that no matter how one tries to be rid of it, there is still always prejudice operating."

"How so?"

"Well, all this time, all the people I've asked about Mrs. Emerson, the postmaster, Taylor Frye, Mrs. Roebuck . . . I don't know how many, it never once occurred to me to ask Mrs. Covington about her. And you know why? Because Mrs. Emerson is white, that's why. I haven't asked anybody who isn't white, and I didn't even realize it until right now."

"And do you suppose," he said, "that Mrs. Covington will give you that same blank stare and say *yes indeed?*"

"She might like to," I said, "but I don't think she will."

If these days were incredible, the nights were even more so, balmy and crisp at the same time. The atmosphere had a sparkling clearness and there was even, to grace it, a full moon. One night Ted and I crossed the bridge and climbed to the top of the red clay bluff to see the town all spread out below us in the moonlight. We had neither of us ever lived any place before that could be seen entirely from one point. To stand there and see it all, all at once, nestled at the bottom of the bowl, the moonlit spray of Chinkapink Creek playing around its feet— it's what always comes to me now whenever I see the word *village* in print.

I needed only the lightest sweater as Ted and I walked up each night after dinner to check up on Joey and Sarah. Sometimes the house was in darkness already and the children would come to the open upstairs windows and, with moonlight shining on their faces, reassure us about their homework, the kitchen stove, even the brushing of their teeth and what had been packed in tomorrow's lunch. All these details I would put in the letter I wrote nightly to their mother. Not that I thought that by reading, on Thursday, that Sarah had worn her plaid blouse to school on Tuesday, or that Joey had been detained in study hall for chewing gum, Mrs. Covington would feel she was getting any useful *news*, but I hoped that the gradual accumulation of the hundreds of minute details would amount to the considerable weight of her being certain that her children were feeling attended and watched over and listened to in her absence.

When I judged that the worst of her postoperative discomfort might be over, I went to the hospital to see Mrs. Covington. She seemed to have shrunk, that was my first impression, as it is almost everybody's, I guess, when they see for the first time a loved person in a hospital bed. I had never known her to dress in white and I found the hospital gown and the stark white sheets a new frame for her face. They brought out her eyes and made them look tremendous. Her skin was given a polished quality. And then of course, quite aside from the effect of the gown, there was the fact that even though she looked more fragile, she also looked rested for the first time in a long time.

"Oh," she said, "I'm so *glad* to see you. I didn't think about your coming. The children? The children all right?"

"They're fine," I said. "I'll tell them all about seeing you to-night."

"Why, then," she said, "you came just for a visit?"

"Sure," I said. "So it's all over? You look wonderful in that hospital gown. You ought to wear white clothes. It does something for your eyes. How are you feeling?"

"I'm feeling so relieved," she said, "and my goodness, I had three of your letters already. They just did me good. Well, I can't talk about that right now. I'll tell you about them later.

118

But anyhow, I want you to know right away. I know you must have been worried is it cancer."

"They did do a biopsy?" I said. I had been afraid to bring this up before.

"They examine under the microscope," she said, "and the laboratory report came back today. It not a cancer."

"That's fine," I said.

"You can believe it," she said. "The doctor know I got two children to provide for. He showed me the report, so I'd believe it myself."

"You're just the opposite of most people I know," I said. "You can talk about cancer naturally; it's love you find so difficult to speak of. Most people now, they talk, talk, talk about love, but *cancer* they're scared to say."

"I got a letter from Albert," she said. "He got his furlough put off all right. He say to concentrate on getting well, just forget everything else. And he try to get here around Easter time."

"Ah, then, everything is lovely," I said. "And, oh yes, I brought you a present from Ted." I took the sealed envelope out of my purse and slid it under her pillow. "Now you must let him do this thing for you, Mrs. Covington. He says nobody ever to his knowledge got to leave a hospital when they thought they would, and he wants you to feel sure you have two extra days."

Her eyes filled with tears and she was quiet, getting herself under control. "I guess the Captain knows," she said, "how much easier it is for me to be proud than gracious. You tell him I . . . well, I thank him. The doctor already told me I can't leave when I planned to. They keep givin me these transfusions. And I can't go back to work, either, the way I thought."

"I'll be sure to tell the children," I said, "so they won't get their hopes set on a particular day. And I think you've had enough excitement. I'm going to leave you now."

"I got a lot to say," she said, "but my heart too full now, I know."

"You save it," I said.

On the way out of the hospital I passed the cart with the thermometers sitting in a beaker of alcohol marked "Colored" beside an identical one marked "white" and I wondered then how far back they carried this foolishness. Did the alcohol, when it was ordered from the supply house, also have to be ordered, "Alcohol, Colored" and "Alcohol, White"? And did the chemist, when he made up his work order, write "C_2H_5OH (Colored)" and "C_2H_5OH (White)"? At any rate, we could be thankful that the doctor seemed just to be practicing medical medicine. And it was a startling measure of what these months in Chinkapink had done to me that I no longer thought of this as a thing one could rightfully expect to take for granted, but instead a thing for which one could be cravenly grateful.

I met Taylor Frye, as we had arranged, in Lawtonville, and rode home with him. Feeling much cheered over my visit with Mrs. Covington, I decided to make blueberry muffins for tea. Though the work had increased so much at the Special Weapons Development Center that Ted was often too late for tea, still we held on to the custom for many reasons. When he did get home in time for it, it meant we could have time in the woods together before dinner without his feeling hungry. In the years before we were married, when I had worked, I had always been ravenous at the end of the day, and had eaten dinner as soon as I could. Somehow for me dinner had always put an end to the working day and, after it, nothing of the day seemed worth the effort to tell it. So I imagined it to be for Ted, whether it really was or not. I hated to be preparing dinner, banging pots and pans, if he had something to tell. To have coffee and a muffin or any slightest thing when he first came home gave us a little time of sitting down together without the urgency of hunger while I heard the news. There was another great advantage and that was sometimes he wanted to bring someone home with him, and to give me warning was almost impossible. We did have a telephone, but the company which owned it was, like the town itself, a local, forgotten thing, slowly dying. One had, from Fort Lassiter, to negotiate with three different local operators. They each had to ring the other and to converse slowly in their thick, thick southern accents, and if they ever succeeded in making the connection, we could then not hear each other because, apparently, all ten of the other parties on the same line had simultaneously taken down their receivers. Because of the fact that our phone also rang for all their calls, we were always stuffing the bell with cotton and forgetting to take it out. So we had a standing arrangement that there would always be coffee and something ready for the unexpected guest and if he then cared to stay to dinner there would be enough edge off his appetite to allow for a trip to Mr. Loftis' Grocery if necessary.

While the muffins were baking, I sprinkled a face towel with a few drops of what we called "Old Mother Demerest's Herbal Tonic," rolled it into a tight cylinder and put it into the old silver butter dish with a little boiling water in the "ice" compartment below. By the time Ted came, the steam would have permeated all through the towel. The sweet herbs I had been so happy to find growing in Mrs. Covington's garden: melissa and lemon verbena and English lavender. These had now steeped in witch hazel in an old green bottle for almost a month, and a few drops on a hot towel into which the face could be buried was enough to wipe out the most frustrating day, or make an interesting one worth telling about. The silver coffeepot steaming, the antique butter dish with its dome cover, the hot muffins wrapped in a napkin—all these I put on the footlocker coffee table, ready. Then I got yesterday's work on the manuscript from Nothing Elaborate and settled down to read it over, placing my chair so that I could see the red oak leaves in the stone jug while they had the last of the evening light. I had had two cups of coffee and two muffins and a cigarette by the time the towel in the butter dish had grown cold and, knowing that Ted had by now missed his ride with Clarence Rochelle and would be coming to Hester on the eight-o'clock bus, I carried the things back to the kitchen and congratulated myself on having saved some of the muffin batter back.

I went down to tell the children good night earlier than usual so that I could give them a good long account of my visit with their mother and to help them through the disappointment of learning she would not be coming home as early as they thought (the day before I had found in Joey's practice typing scraps: *Mrs. Demerest, be glad you alive*). On the way back, I stopped in Mr. Loftis' store to report on my visit to the hospital. For the first time I saw him forget all about his customers, his store, everything, in his eagerness to hear every possible detail, and, as his face lost the smiling, cheerful manner he had for customers and became suffused with attention and concern, I saw how very much they looked alike, Serena and her father.

I stayed longer than I had planned, and, as I hurried the preparations for dinner, knowing Ted must by now be off the bus and started on the two-mile walk, I suddenly was startled out of my skin by the sound of a siren. An air raid drill *here?* I stepped onto the back porch and I could see the lights going out in all the houses, so I went in quickly and turned off the kerosene stove and snapped off all the lights. Taylor Frye had told me that among his many other duties he was the air raid warden and I knew he would surely take it extra hard if a violator turned out to be his own tenant. So, conscientiously, I turned out the last light, wondering how, possibly, this small, forgotten place of no military importance whatever could take its danger seriously enough to satisfy a personality like Taylor Frye's, and I found myself absolutely helpless in my own house. I could not remember how far it was to any known thing in the room I stood in or, if I moved, what I might run into. The moon, which had been so lovely a few nights ago, was now dark, and there was no glow of any kind at the windows. I think I had never been in such absolute darkness. I found it stifling, and, completely disoriented, I now groped for the nearest wall and, taking inch steps, crept along it until I had a doorknob

122

in my hands. Once in the front hall, though it seemed to me that it took hours, I did finally find the front door of the building and, opening it, I held one foot out cautiously because I could not now remember if there was a step down onto the porch. I had already stumbled over an uneven floor board in the hall and nearly fallen. On the porch, I leaned against the closed front door and waited until my eyes should adapt to the darkness, but they did not. There was no glow from the sky, no outline of the hills, there was only blackness. I shuffled across the porch and managed to avoid the pit of the front steps and to find my hand on the banister. At last I could see stars. Never have I seen them so bright, so close. But I could see nothing else. Always before in air raid drills we had been in a city where there were some lights left or a movement of cars with covered headlights. And never had there been this quiet. As I learned later, no one in Chinkapink had blackout curtains or made the slightest effort for continuing activity in an air raid drill. At the sound of the siren everybody simply turned out the stove and the lights and went to bed and slept until the next morning. Now I could hear the sound of the kerosene stoves all over the town, slowly and erratically sounding off in this natural echo chamber as air bubbles worked their way up through the fuel. It was like being transplanted to a desolate volcanic region where small mudpots pushed up, unrhythmically, their gluey bubbles, one by one.

The unearthly quiet was split with the sound of a motor starting up and a siren moving through the streets and away, and NOW I remembered that Taylor Frye had told me he always took the ambulance in an air raid drill and drove it with the siren going to his "station" in Hester. "I'm allowed to have the lights on if I have blue paper over them," he had said, "but it's too much trouble. I know that road by heart, every curve in it. I can drive it at sixty miles an hour in the dark." *And right now, surely, Ted was on that road, on foot.*

I started in my panic for the stairs, but a moment of groping in mid-air sobered me up and made me realize how impossible it was that I could catch the ambulance. What good would it do Ted to find me with my head busted open on the worn, rough bricks of the streets of Chinkapink? Was there nothing, nothing I could do? I prayed that when he heard the siren he would throw himself into the ditch and that if he walked as far as the town, where he would have to make turns to our house, I could call out and guide him by my voice.

The hot, coppery taste of fear ran into my mouth as the sound of the siren became fainter and fainter and at last ceased altogether. It seemed an eternity after that when, over the sound of my own heart beating, I heard Ted's step echoing back from the hills. He was alive, but I did not see how. I called out and had no answer. Wait now, I said to myself. He's made it this far. Don't try to go to him; you'll only fall. Finally in the distance (but what distance I had no reference for) I saw a blue glow shimmering in the air. All the stories that I had ever heard of will-o'-the-wisps, ghosts of bad men, of marsh lights, suddenly came back to me. I tried to ignore this because I could still hear the footsteps and *they* were real, I thought. At last my call got an answer. The blue light, which had a moment before been miles away, now seemed to be in our own yard.

"Here," Ted said, very close to me. "Here. Where are the damned steps?"

I reached a hand down to him and caught hold of his shoulder. He stumbled up the steps. "Don't touch me," he said. "Get a can or a pan or anything. Get these damned things off me."

"But what is it?" I said, for now I could see the line of his chin etched into the darkness.

"Glowworms," he said. "They're crawling all over me."

We made it into the house and by the light of his hands and his chin we groped our way to the kitchen. I found an empty coffee can and we began picking the bugs off him and putting them into the can, where they slid about like children on new roller skates, and I collapsed in hysterical laughter.

124

"I thought you would be killed," I said. "I heard Taylor Frye tear out of here in that ambulance and I knew you were on that road. Oh, I was so frightened."

"So was I," he said. "Of course the bus had to stop and it was right at our road, so rather than sit there for hours I decided to get out and walk. It never occurred to me there would be anything moving on our road. Of course I had forgotten about Taylor Frye and his ambulance. I heard the motor start up and that siren and it dawned on me he'd be coming around those curves trying to prove how fast he could do it, so I dived into the bushes and got two handfuls of glowworms and held them under my chin. I didn't have time to do anything else."

"Did he see you?"

"Well, he swerved," Ted said. "I don't know what he thinks he saw, but he swerved. And thank God, there was no one else behind him."

We sat on the kitchen floor by the strange blue light reflected from the tin of the coffee can, too exhausted to get up until the all clear sounded.

"It would take someone like Taylor Frye," Ted said, "to make a hazard out of what must geographically be the safest spot in the whole country."

The next morning the ground was covered with frost and the strange false spring weather was at an end, making even more miraculous the glowworms whose preserving light Ted had found on their last possible night. Otherwise, it was a day of returns, for Benedict was at the back door soon after breakfast, carrying in the ice as though he had never been away. I barely recognized him, for he was bareheaded, and so much was his big black pirate hat a part of him I could not remember ever having seen him without it.

"How nice to see you, Benedict," I said. "We missed you."

"Yes, ma'am," he said. He bent down and pulled the pan from under the icebox.

"You see, it's not overflowing. I had to learn to remember when you were gone."

He carried the pan over to the sink, emptied it carefully and replaced it. "Don't lift it ever again," he said. "From now on, I empty it for you, remember."

It was somehow as though *I* had been in jail and must now be compensated for it. "Oh, Benedict, how was it really? Was it pretty bad? We . . ."

"Why, no, Mrs. Demerest," he said. "It was all right. Onliest thing, somebody taken my hat. I had that hat for years. I don't know can I find another like it."

"Oh, Benedict," I said, and outside in the truck I could feel the presence of Redley Stuart waiting for me to "get all upset." "Benedict, I'm so sorry about your hat."

He turned upon me such a look of sympathy, all wordless, that I felt complete defeat and knew that it was actually possible I might find myself trying to convince Benedict that, really, it was not I who had been inconvenienced. He opened the screen and jumped from the back porch onto the rear of the truck. Redley Stuart, driving, waved to me as the truck moved off. There was no mistaking how he felt; *he* was a happy man.

Also, this day, Mrs. Wilkie returned with Gary Cooper, Joan Crawford and Rita Hayworth. Fortunately, I saw the taxi in front of the house and I ran as fast as I could into the bathroom and snatched down the towel and washcloth I had just put up for Wilkie. I didn't feel up to taking on Mrs. Wilkie just now, especially if, as I thought it likely, she had had to return because, wherever she had gone, they would not take her. Nor could I face the prospect of another night sitting up past midnight while we heard *her* life history.

Quite enough of her history could be read in the following weeks from the trash can which we shared in common. Bottles of Lydia Pinkham, Nervina and Quieten bore their testimony, sometimes quite beautifully covered with needles of frost as the weather became progressively crisper and colder.

11

ONE EVENING Ted brought Lee Carter Higgins home with him to tea, and the likes of this our living room had never experienced before. He was, at one glance, unmistakably a prince. He was beautiful and he glowed and radiated pure happiness. His black hair was mussed into small, rebellious ringlets. His eyes were crystalline blue. He was not as tall as Ted, but in perfect proportion. His hands were slender and hard to the touch. His feet were elegantly shod in soft brown shoes of an extraordinary narrowness. His forehead (really, at the first glance I thought of it as a "brow") was high and narrow without seeming at all pinched, and in his very first words of greeting, spoken in a beautiful voice, he proclaimed himself, in the way of a highly bred animal or of a sensitively conceived work of art, as extraordinarily alive. Here, certainly, was the very embodiment of the word *aristocrat*, and it was suffused with a crackling, sparkling delight.

Lee Carter Higgins was delighted with the hot towel out of the antique butter dish and instantly identified two of the herbs.

I had made scones that night and, though I knew it could not be true, I was shortly believing that he was a man who might have died if he had not had a hot scone by nightfall. He penetrated almost immediately to the very essence of the roots box, and I heard Ted telling him of it with a gaiety and wit that made my husband a fascinating stranger to me. Ted introduced Lee Carter formally to Nothing Elaborate and even took him into the bedroom to meet Halfway Decent. It was hard for me to leave the room even long enough to get fresh scones, I was so fascinated, and I could not have said which of them fascinated me the more, the newcomer or the delightful creature he had suddenly made out of my husband. For a moment I felt a weight on my heart, for is it I, I thought, who makes him so serious, so gently sad?

Then suddenly Lee Carter Higgins was saying his charming good-bys and he could not stay for dinner because his wife "at the place," he said, would be waiting dinner for him. And he was gone.

"Is he real?" I said to Ted. "And where on earth did you find him?"

"Why, he works at Special Weapons," Ted said. "He's a civilian employed on some special assignment there. He's always very polite, but I had no idea he was like this. He's so quiet there. Nobody knows anything about him. Several people told me he was an Englishman, and it's not true. On the way home he told me he lives about thirty miles from here in his own house. He does some very specialized work, alone. He doesn't work with anybody else. Tonight we happened to be coming out at the same time and he said since he had to go in this direction couldn't he carry me home. I told him I had to let Clarence know, so he insisted on taking me over to where I meet Clarence, and waiting for me while I explained. Of course, now you've seen him, you can understand how he gave me the impression that I was conferring a special favor on him to allow him to bring me home."

"Funny thing," I said. "Lee Carter Higgins doesn't seem to have any age. He could be twenty or thirty-five or . . ."

"He's forty-two," Ted said. "He happened to mention it on the way home."

Sarah took with her usual equanimity the news that her mother's homecoming would be delayed and listened attentively to my account of my visit at the hospital, but Joey, being younger, was unable to hide the strain of this extra wait. A very slight stammer came back into his speech almost immediately. I wasn't alarmed, because I had myself stupidly brought it on early in our acquaintance by making him self-conscious about saying *yes ma'am* to me and demanding that he call me Molly, a thing too hard for him to do. But, as I had taken pains to remedy this and as we had become friends, the stammer wore off. I had not heard it for a long time and I was even now almost grateful to have such a clear indication to go by without having to guess how he was taking this news. It was perfectly clear that the delay was an amount of strain that, for the moment, was a little too much. In his need to strike out at something—he could not of course blame his mother; he dared not blame me—he picked on Sarah's lunches as the explanation of his discontent. They were all the same, he said, and now in memory the lunches his mother had made for him were regular feasts.

It was, fortunately, a thing I could easily do something about, and so I said I thought Sarah was maybe tired of getting them and that, since she did all the washing and ironing and house-cleaning on top of her homework, I would get their lunches for a few days.

It was not a matter of life and death; still, I did think it was rather important to put some imagination into the first (Monday's) lunch. So when Ted came home Saturday evening with Lee Carter Higgins, who said, "Grab a toothbrush. I'm taking you both home for dinner and to spend the night," I did make sure that Higgins said it was "nothing at all" to bring us back for sure on Sunday. While I was packing the "toothbrush"—after all, it was a chance for Ted to wear civilian clothes for a change—Ted went out the back door and down to tell either Sarah or Mr. Loftis or both that we would be away that night, so we could set our minds at ease.

As we drove further and further into the country on a labyrinth of twisting, turning country roads, I felt a mild sense of alarm, for had either of us known how inaccessible the place was, I don't suppose we would have so blithely dashed off on Higgins' promise that it would be "no trouble at all" to get us back when we wanted to come. We did rapidly gain an appreciation of what Redley Stuart had meant, though, when he said the roads were really deplorable.

Lee Carter Higgins had to keep his attention on the road, but he kept his good nature and was apologetic over the worst bumps. Suddenly he announced that we were now on Bewelcome's acres and that to our left was the picnic ground. A little further on he pointed out the summerhouse, the slave cemetery, the woodland. There was nothing at any of these places but raw, red earth (except for the woodland—there were a few scraggly pines). I thought it a joke and turned to him, smiling, but he was looking at me with cold, strange eyes, *daring* me to say I did not see any summerhouse. His voice now changed, became somber, heavier, humorless, as he explained the plans for restoring the whole place exactly as it had once been. No, he said, it had not been his own home, that had been a few miles away, but this place had belonged to worthless cousins who had let it go to pieces, until finally the last of them had died two years ago, and he had been able to buy the place cheap. "Why, the house," he said, "it was a shambles. One whole wall had fallen out. You never saw such a wreck." He and his wife had had to tackle the house first, and then the barn, to the neglect of other things.

Slowly the car crept over the bare, red dirt in the last of the evening light. It seemed much more like some mesa in Arizona than any part of the South. We met no people. "But what happened to it?" Ted said. "It can't have been drought."

"Tobacco," Lee Carter said. "Nothing but tobacco, the fools. It'll take years and years to get it back to what it was. We have pictures, you know, of everything. Part of the original house dates from 1700. We even have documents for the original colors of the walls inside, so that we were able to restore exactly. Even the designs of the original hardware are recorded. Bewelcome was a showplace once. There was quite a lot written about it because it was one of the few that survived the battle. It was fired once, but it was all brick, and besides, *that* was one we won, so the house had attention right away."

"Always tobacco?" Ted said, for he could not get over the terrible ravaged look of the land.

"Oh, no," Lee Carter said. "It was a breeding farm originally."

"Cattle?" I said. "Or horses?"

"Why, no," Lee Carter said. "Slaves. Bewelcome was a slave-breeding farm."

I felt Ted's hand tighten on my shoulder, and I was glad to have it there, but if he feared that I was going to speak out in haste, he was mistaken. I was speechless. Of course, as a child, I knew that slaves were sold. I knew about boats that brought slaves from Africa. Once a year on Abraham Lincoln's birthday somebody gave a speech in school, but after I was old enough to know where babies came from I never seemed to have thought slavery through these literal details. The emphasis had all been on the selling. It astounded me that one could really have spent considerable time thinking, reading and talking about civil rights and actually never have stumbled across the reality of breeding human beings for money. Certainly, if I had thought it through, I would have thought that any descendant of a slave "breeder" would not care to boast of it.

Then Lee Carter stopped the car the better for us to appreciate the difference in the landscape, for now came the sharp line of the land that had been reclaimed, the signs of beautiful order

that seemed to be spreading out from its center, which was Bewelcome, the house itself, a noble and simple, beautiful structure
of red brick with white painted trim, and lights at the windows.
After the desolation we had seen, the effect was breath-taking.

"I'm so sorry the daylight's gone," Lee Carter said, "but then
in the morning I'll show you around."

Our eyes had been so drawn to the house that we had not been
aware of the gate across the road. A white man in overalls and
a big straw hat came hurrying up to open the gate. He touched
his hat to Lee Carter. "Evenin, sir," he said. "Evening," Lee
Carter said, and we drove through the gate.

"That was a nice feudal touch," Ted said. "What is he, a
movie prop?"

"Who? Oh, my man," Lee Carter said. "He's a very good
man. Stubborn, though. Pigheaded."

The front door opened into a center hall of simple beauty
and we were met immediately by the odor of fresh wax and
lemon oil. The floor was bare, of wide, random-length pine
boards, polished to a beautiful warm sheen. "All these boards,"
Lee Carter said. "Almost all of them had to be replaced. They
were all rotted. Big holes in them. Oh, we worked, I'll tell you.
And of course," he said, leading us to where we could see the
very simple and beautiful curve of the stairway, over which was
draped a Confederate flag, "you know what that is." He stood
perfectly still and looked up at the flag as though he had just
finished draping it there with much satisfaction.

"What's the proper thing?" Ted said. "Are we supposed to
genuflect, now?"

"Just have the grace to blush," Lee Carter said. Then, for a
moment, he became recognizable in his manner, taking our wraps
and leading us into a large room off the hall where there was a
giant log burning in a fireplace that took up an entire wall. "Sit
down," he said. "I'll get you a drink and tell Myra we're here."

It was a beautiful room, done with quiet feeling. There were
recessed bookshelves with worn, used books in them. There was

132

no excess of decoration, the simplest lines prevailing. The only light was from giant candles set into the walls. There was a huge brass bowl on the coffee table, filled with chrysanthemums. Just under the odor of the fire and the chrysanthemums and the wax, there was—not a real odor—but certainly the awareness of soap. What mountains of soap and scrub brushes it must have taken, I thought.

Lee Carter came back alone, carrying drinks on a tray. He had changed into a smoking jacket and his face looked freshly scrubbed. He made no mention of his wife and sat sipping his wine and looking into the fire. Then with sudden animation he turned to me. "We've a newborn calf," he said. "The sweetest thing. After dinner I'll show him to you. There'll be a moon then. The barn is beautiful by moonlight. I bought the cow at auction. This is her first calf." Then, to Ted, he said: "You'd love the auctions. You ought to go sometime. I take my man with me. He's good about stock. All the gentlemen take their men." He was perfectly straight-faced about it. I had no idea there was anyone in America who used the word *gentleman* in that sense and Lee Carter himself could surely not have been without some awareness of what we were thinking, for though neither of us made any comment, he said, "Oh, it's all very democratic, really. Except, of course, when Colonel Buckley invites the gentlemen over to his car for a drink, the men know better than to come."

Slowly our hunger mounted. We could hear someone moving about in the next room, which, by the sounds of plates being put down, silverware being laid, identified itself as a dining room. The step was rapid but heavy. Finally Lee Carter called out: "Myra, can't you stop and come in now?"

"No, I can NOT," a woman's voice said. It was not a southern accent and the tone was decidedly angry. Suddenly I realized that we had not been expected. Now, terribly hungry and up against a man who spoke as though he had been alive in the Civil War, we were miles from transportation, stuck here overnight in the house of a woman who didn't want us and was angry before she had ever seen us. What's more, if I drank one more glass of wine without food I would be tight.

Lee Carter made no answer to the woman. He stood his ground, he poured more wine, he went right on telling of the restoration of the house, and of how they had found the original English wallpaper in one of the upstairs rooms. Ted, walking about the room (as he told me later, he was trying to mask the growling of his empty stomach with footsteps), examined the old maps on the wall which showed, as Lee Carter pointed out, the battles "we" had won and those "we" had lost. Finally, from the dining room, we heard the firm steps approaching and Myra came in.

My heart went out to her in instant sympathy. She wore no make-up, her hair was not "done." She had on a cotton house-dress. Her rather thick, short legs were bare and she had on "sensible" oxfords with walking heels (these had made the heavy steps). She was a very plain woman who thought herself ugly and she was over fifty. One look at her and one was instantly reminded how very costly princes are.

"Did you have any more warning than we did?" I said.

"Well, really less," she said, and then something in her decided not to go on with it, this heavy sullen hatred, and she laughed in an acceptance of everything.

"Can't I come to the kitchen with you?" I said.

"All right," she said, and she turned and left the room.

Once inside the kitchen, I was immediately oriented. It was a kitchen organized on pure logic, nothing useless or "cute" in it, neither was it a "dream kitchen" in the sense of labor-saving equipment. It was beautiful in itself for the way that nothing was in the way of anything else. It was clear that all stages of the dinner were in progress and under control and I saw that the most helpful thing I could do would be to wash the dishes used in cooking which would be in the way of the dishing up. So I went to the sink, washed my hands and began to clean the dishes

134

off with a brush under the tap. I saw Myra watching me. She said nothing. When the dishes were all rinsed and organized, I reached for the soap, which was not only where I reached but turned out to be Fels Naphtha Flakes. This, my own favorite, I had long been unable to find, and I said how pleased I was. Since there was a teakettle, I assumed that she wished the dishes scalded, so I filled the kettle so that it would be hot when I needed it. At this, Myra handed me an apron. It was the simplest, clearest message of acceptance. Now I myself prefer to do dishes in this way. However, if I'm in a house where they habitually wash them with pieces of garbage in the suds, it doesn't give me a neurosis. What upsets *me* is the changing of a word like "victory" to mean "ersatz" without any previous agreement about it.

On the shelf above the sink there were pots of basil, thyme, tarragon and chives. "No wonder Lee Carter recognized the herbs at our house," I said. She made no comment and I realized that he did not discuss with her where he had been.

"This soap," I said. "It is to me the cleanest smell in the world. You know, in the grocery in Chinkapink" (it had been in Roebuck's) "I heard one woman tell another she used 'sweet soap' for washing dishes in order to protect her hands, and that her husband had complained the stew tasted of Lux. I'd never heard the expression before."

"All southern women are lazy," Myra said, "and dirty. I haven't seen one yet who isn't."

"Myra," I said, "could I please have a bite of bread or sugar?"

"Why, of course," she said, as she reached into the bread box and brought out a loaf of whole-wheat bread with pan marks on it.

"Homemade?"

"Why, yes," she said. "Our own wheat ground in our own mill right here. It was mean of me not to send in anything with the wine. I'm really sorry."

It was wonderful bread. "Oh, Ted must taste this," I said.

135

"I'll be right back." I went into the room where I had left Ted and Lee Carter, bread extended. "Ted," I said, "you must taste. It's homemade and they even have their own mill." He turned upon me a glazed look of gratitude composed of starvation and alcohol, and unobtrusively wolfed down the bread.

"We certainly do have our own mill," Lee Carter said. "Myra was determined to make the thing run. I don't suppose it had been working for at least fifty years. The course of the stream had changed so it didn't even go by the mill; we had to deflect it. That is, *I* had to deflect it."

Then Myra was there, saying dinner was ready. It was a superb dinner, and when you considered that she had to start it after we got there, it was an amazing accomplishment. When we complimented her, though, she said, "Lee Carter says he hasn't had a decent meal since we moved here."

"Well," he said, "she won't let me buy anything in a store. Everything on the table came from the place, and it gets monotonous."

"It's the only way to make a place self-supporting," Myra said. "Of course Lee Carter read an article on food poisoning and now refuses to eat any of the five hundred quarts of vegetables I canned."

"Do you mean," Ted said to her, "that you have not only restored the house but reconditioned enough land in a year and a half to make this place self-supporting?"

"Oh, no," she said. "It will be five years yet. Then, if we don't have to hire my labor done (I realize I may not last at this pace forever) the place can begin to make a profit or we can get another piece of land conditioned."

"Do you do everything yourself?" I asked. "Without help?"

"Myra hates niggers," Lee Carter said, "even though she is a Yankee."

"I won't have one on the place," she said. "They're lazy and dirty. Of course," she added, "I must say I feel just the same

136

about the whites here. The wife of Lee Carter's man can't even be trusted to sterilize the milk cans."

"But, Myra, I tell you over and over, she *has* to do what you tell her. Just see that she does."

"She would only lie to me," Myra said. "In two months she wouldn't learn to read a thermometer for pasteurizing the milk. If I have to stand over her, I might as well do it."

The house must have fifteen rooms, I thought. How was it possible for her to do all this without any help whatever, on top of the farm work? And to a person so overworked, how must we two unexpected dinner guests have appeared? I never in my life so wanted to leave a place. Surely we could get away early the next day.

"We never did have house niggers," Lee Carter said. "Even when Bewelcome was a slave-breeding place, we never had them in the house. We always had indentured servants."

Myra turned to Ted. "He doesn't distinguish the centuries," she said. "You'll get used to it in time."

"It's such a mess now. It's terrible what's happened with the niggers," Lee Carter said, "and it will take a terrible amount of money to put things right, but it's the only thing to do."

"What?" Ted said. "You have some solution in mind?"

"Why, they'll have to be sent back," he said, "every damned one of them, that's all."

"Back *where?*" I said.

"Why, Africa, of course," he said. "There's nothing else to do."

"*Africa?* Why, American Negroes don't have any . . ." The preposterousness of it simply overcame me and I couldn't go on. "Damnedest thing I ever heard," I said.

"There's nothing else to do," he said. "Of course *now* they have an understanding. No matter what they say in Washington, the niggers understand it means nothing. They understand they don't vote. But how long will that last? I've talked to people in the state legislature and in the state government, too, and we all know. It's all understood. If they try to *vote*, we're ready for them. But you can't shoot them *all*; it's much better, before that happens, just to send them back, no matter what it costs."

Myra stood up to clear the table then and Ted, seeing the serving tray was large and heavy, carried it out to the kitchen for her. After dessert we went out to see the calf. Lee Carter soothed the cow and she let him sit by the little calf. Here was again the black-haired prince (a child prince now), lovely and gentle and filled with delight. I was filled with delight myself, for now I too sat on the stable floor and put my head close to the calf's and smelled its sweet smell. Later, with the horses, Lee Carter was the same: affectionate, loving and gentle. Yet, inside the house again, as though the Confederate flag emanated some poison for him as he passed it, he was immediately transformed. His walk, his posture, the expression of his eyes, even his voice, changed instantly.

Myra came in and sat with us. Knowing she must have had to arise at five or six o'clock, I did not see how she could possibly hold her eyes open, but she seemed to grow every minute more rested and alert. And now her past history came into the picture. She had, for many years, been an executive in a large business. She had never cooked before, never kept house, had learned all these things out of desperation that there was no one else to do them. They had traveled a great deal in connection with her business. She spoke several languages, apparently with ease. Finding Ted had been interested in her seven-year plan, which he had seen outlined in the farm office off the kitchen, she now spoke of co-operative farming in Denmark. Ted had read of it and began asking her questions. By the thoroughness of her answers and her quickness to interpret his questions, one suddenly saw, as a blaze of light, the keenness of her mind.

Lee Carter grew progressively more restless as Myra and Ted found themselves in further pleasant agreement about co-operative farming. "It won't work," he said.

"What won't?" Ted said.

"Co-operative farming," he said. "It won't work."

"But that's what we have just been saying," Myra said, "that it does work in Denmark."

"It won't work," he said.

Myra sighed in exasperation, but there was no real anger in it. It was more a gesture of defeat.

"Take my man," Lee Carter said. "I gave him two cows. He won't keep them with mine. I've explained all the advantages to him a hundred times of keeping them together. No, he won't. He wants his separate. He's pigheaded. Stubborn."

"Why do you *persist?*" Myra said, and now suddenly there was real anger flashing out. "Why do you *persist* in ignoring the issue?"

"The issue is he won't keep his cows with mine," Lee Carter said, "because he's stubborn."

"It is NOT," she said, "and you know it perfectly well. Why do you continue to ignore the point? You have to settle the essential point and come to agreement on it." Then, turning to Ted, she said, "You see, one of the cows is going to calf, and the man thinks the calf should belong to him."

"That's absurd," Lee Carter said. "The calf belongs to me, of course."

"It isn't *of course* to him," Myra said. "Why don't you settle it?"

"It's settled," he said. "Everybody knows the calves belong to the gentleman. That has nothing to do with it. He's just stubborn."

"Doesn't the cow have anything to say about it at all?" I said. "After all, it's her calf."

"How delightful," Lee Carter said, suddenly laughing. "You have such a charming idea of justice. It's what I'll do. I'll make the man ask the cow."

Somehow this put me in the position of being Lee Carter's ally. I had got him out of this thing and, by his gay manner, he showed that this was his victory, that he had made me help him.

Never did I want less to be an ally, and never did I feel more my inexperience with princes. I retreated, defeated, to bed.

Nowhere does a well-run farm show itself so perfectly to city people as at breakfast. The home-cured ham, the hours-fresh eggs, the butter fresh from the churn—especially the taste of the butter, so delicious that in order to relish it the more one refuses the homemade preserves.

As soon as decently possible, we spoke of returning home.

"Home?" Lee Carter said. "Why, what are you talking about? We're enjoying your company. We want you to stay overnight."

"Oh, no," Ted said. "We only planned to stay the one night. Of course I didn't realize the distance when you assured us it would be no trouble at all to bring us back today, but if it is inconvenient for you, perhaps you can get us to a highway bus."

"Why, no," Lee Carter said. "I won't have you feeling it's an inconvenience." A look of great innocence came over his face. "But I thought it was all understood you'd be here for the week-end."

"Oh, no," I said. "Why, I made a particular point of it, don't you remember? I couldn't have come at all otherwise. I've promised to get back."

"I certainly couldn't let you go until you've seen the place by daylight. There's so much to show you. Come on. Come on." He became very bustling and cheerful, talking about future plans. I looked toward Myra, hoping she would say, "Oh, I can run you in," or "Of course, he'll take you if you must go," but she avoided my eyes. Nor did she come with us for the "tour."

And always the next thing we must see was a little further on. Lee Carter was clever and skillful, but not quite skillful enough to hide the fact that he was stalling for time, but we had no inkling of what could possibly have justified all this urgency. I had the feeling of being in an old fairytale. Soon we would come to the forest and he would lure us in a circular path and then abandon us. Fortunately, there was no forest, and Ted finally turned resolutely toward the house. But Lee Carter had been saving his best for last and, sure that *this* would hold us fascinated, he steered us toward it.

"And here," he said, "is the most valuable thing of all historically—the breeding pens." We came to what appeared at first to be rubble. A disintegrating structure was hinted in the brick floor and remnants of a low foundation. One could make out partitions in various states of decay that had defined spaces like stalls. "Oh yes," Lee Carter said, "I want to restore this, exactly as it was. See here, here's one of the old chains. They were bolted into the walls. This may be the only breeding pen still left in this state; that is, I haven't heard of any others. A few more years, if we hadn't got the place, and it might have been gone completely."

"Well, yes," I said, "I should think people would have been eager to get them out of sight and covered over."

"Not at all," Lee Carter said. "Why, it's fascinating. You know, Bewelcome once had a bull slave that could service forty cow slaves in . . . Well, I know you're a Yankee girl and real broadminded and all, but . . ." He turned to Ted and began to mutter behind his hand. I was glad to be spared, and used the slack in the leash of his attention to make more progress toward the house.

Once inside, I went to our room to collect our things. As I came downstairs, Ted and Lee Carter were just entering and I went resolutely to the hall closet and got our coats.

"Now, here," Lee Carter said, "what are you doing spoiling everything? You're going to stay for lunch with us, at least. . . ."

"No," I said, "we have to get back. We really do."

"But," he said, "how can you? You're my prisoners. I won't let you go. Now I've got you here, and you know you could never find your way out of here."

"Well, we can walk, I guess," Ted said. "I don't suppose you could be trusted to point out the right road, though. What's the great value of our presence, Lee Carter? Did Myra have the deflecting of another stream bed planned for this weekend?"

"Oh, now, I was only teasing about holding you prisoners," Lee Carter said. "Of course if you have to go . . . But let's all have a glass of sherry first. I know you wouldn't go without saying good-by to Myra."

"Of course not," I said.

"Well, sit down, then. You make me feel you don't like our hospitality. I'll go get Myra and a little glass of sherry for us."

Feeling this was the moment to be patient, since victory was practically ours, we sat down. It was, after all, a great deal more to ask of a man on his one day off than we had thought when we asked it. Soon Myra came in. She wore jeans and a shirt and she had taken some pains with her hair. All at once I could see how she might have been quite handsome—well-tailored, scrubbed, brushed, clear-eyed and confident. Lee Carter, emanating cheer and good will, brought in the sherry. I invited Myra to come in and spend a day with me.

"I'd like that," she said. "What day is best for you?"

I was surprised at her response and suddenly I realized that she went nowhere. "Why, any day at all," I said. "You could come in with Lee Carter in the morning and he could pick you up in the evening. We could go to the woods."

"Can't you stay for lunch?" she said.

"Oh, no," I said. "Really, we do have to get back. I've promised to."

"Oh," she said, "I didn't realize you had a definite engagement."

"Yes," I said, "a friend of mine is in the hospital and I've promised to get her little boy's school lunch. I haven't even shopped for the food yet, and I did want to fix him something special."

"But it's such a little town," she said. "Can't he come to your home for lunch?"

142

"Why, no," I said. "He goes to school in Montrose and leaves at six in the morning. He'd be twelve hours without food."

"Montrose?" Lee Carter said. "You mean he's a nigger child?"

"He's colored, yes," I said.

"The very idea," Lee Carter said. "Why, the little bastard. I've a mind to . . ." His face became apoplectic with fury and his eyes glared insanely. "Expecting you, *you* to get his lunch. The nerve . . ."

"You have it all wrong," I said. "It was my idea, not the boy's. I volunteered this and I don't want to break my promise." I turned away from him and spoke to Myra. "You know, the mother's had a serious operation and her homecoming's been postponed. It's hard on a child. . . ."

"Then you don't have to go," Lee Carter said. "I'm so glad. I thought it was something important." He was now quite relaxed, had poured himself another sherry.

"Yes, I *do* have to go," I said.

"Why," he laughed, "just buy him a penny's worth of candy tomorrow. He'll like that much better."

I started to say, *His grandfather's store is full of candy*, and realized that I was afraid, really afraid, to identify Joey. I thought back frantically. Had I used his name? Had I said, *my friend Mrs. Covington?*

"I doubt if he could be fooled by that," Ted said. "He's a very bright little boy."

"Bright?" Lee Carter said. "Yes, of course he's bright. They are, you know. They're much brighter than white children up to the age of eight, and then they start to regress."

"You aren't serious?" I said.

"Why, of course," he said. "Everybody knows that."

"Is this Bewelcome's very own brand of anthropology," I said, "or did you learn this in a university?"

"Have another sherry," he said. "And now of course you'll stay to lunch."

It was my turn to get apoplectic. But Ted just held my coat

143

for me. "What you don't understand, Higgins," he said, "is her promises. I do. Now we have to go." And he put on his own coat and went over to Myra to say good-by.

"But I won't *have* it," Lee Carter said, and he actually stamped his foot. "The idea of taking a promise to a little nigger bastard seriously . . ."

"Listen," I said, "*I* made the promise and the promise has no color at all."

"Myra," Ted said, "which is the road we take?"

Just then the doorbell rang and Lee Carter, hoping yet this would be something for his side, laughed and ran to answer it. It turned out to be Lieutenant and Mrs. Johnson, who were out for a ride and had just dropped by, as Lee Carter, they said, had been urging them to do, only they had used up all their time trying to find the place.

"Are you going back to Lawtonville?" Ted said to Lieutenant Johnson.

"Yes," he said. "Can we give you a lift?"

"If you would," Ted said. "Then Lee Carter wouldn't have to take us. We'd appreciate it."

We were now of no importance to Higgins; the Johnsons were. Upon them he focused all his attention and presence. They also had a glass of sherry and they, too, were urged to stay to lunch. Lee Carter was all relaxed charm, now. It was clear that he felt well able to overcome them and he gave me a quick glance of malice to show his anticipated triumph. But it turned out that the Johnsons had a baby whose sleep was being watched over by a neighbor and the baby's waking time was soon. Even Lee Carter Higgins knew better than to try to buy off somebody's own white baby with a penny's worth of candy. And so, very soon, we four were walking out the door. So free did I feel to be out of this trap that I could barely restrain myself from running. As we were actually moving through the door, Lee Carter's resistance suddenly collapsed. He became the charming prince again, helpful about how the car should be turned around, courteous, inviting us all to come back.

Inside the car I prayed, *Start the motor, start the motor*. Lee Carter stepped back and waved to us. He was smiling his most beautiful smile. Then he moved up to the window and said to me, "But that's not a Yankee conscience you have, you know. That's a southern conscience."

"Oh, go to hell," I said. "Go to hell."

12

MY SCHOOL LUNCH career only lasted three days and then on the afternoon of the third day Joey was there to tell me (one look at his face was all I needed) that his mother was home. Although she had to stay in bed, I knew now that Joey would find no fault with Sarah, nor would he like his mother to know he ever had. The slight stammer was miraculously gone. I sent his mother a note and made Joey promise to tell me how she was each day and I planned to stay out of the way until she was rested, but in the store Mr. Loftis told me Serena would like for me to come see her. So in a few days I was once again sitting by her bed and we were talking and waiting for her to get well and making plans about going to the woods.

"I hold on to that," she said, "when I get discouraged. The doctor say I can't work in the store till he tells me. I thought I'd be back at work by now. But when I get impatient, I make myself think about that trip to the woods we gone take together. I remember places I hadn't thought of for years and certain plants to show you. There's a kind of moss has little red flowers. But then, that was under the snow."

"Snow?" I said. "Does it snow here?"

"Not every year," she said. "But sometimes it does. I love the snow. Sometime there's ice, too, and the trees all covered with it. I remember once, you know that magnolia tree by the old mill? Well, it was all covered with ice and suddenly the ice start to melt and fall off and it was leaves, perfect leaves of ice with the veins and everything on them. They so beautiful."

"Say, I've been meaning to ask you. You know that Mrs. Emerson, that old woman? Well, I met her one day when I was out walking up by her old house and I've been asking people ever since and they just give me a glassy stare and say *yes indeed* and that's all. Then one day when you were in the hospital, she came in your father's store. So I realized you must know her story."

Serena lowered her eyelids and with one of her long, thin hands she smoothed the bedspread. "Ah, poor thing," she said. "I sorry you ever saw her the way she is."

"Was she much different once? I noticed your father treated her with such kindness, I felt she must once have been . . . well, very different."

Serena's hand doubled into a fist and she pounded it against the bed a couple of times. She threw her head back against the pillow and, her eyes closed, moved her head restlessly from side to side.

"If it disturbs you," I said, "we'd better wait. I . . . ."

"She was the most beautiful person," she said. "You can't imagine, I know, seeing her this way. But she was. And the loveliest manner. The way she spoke to the children on the street: *Hello, dear,* she say. *Hello, darling.* And her smile. She look right at you and smile right at you. *How are you today?* she say. She had the loveliest smile I ever saw and the most beautiful eyes. She was . . . she was happy. She made you happy, just to be near her."

I thought of Mrs. Emerson's eyes, bleary and mad under strings of gray, greasy hair. It was hard to believe that she could ever have been beautiful, though after the resurrection of it I had seen in the Loftis Grocery, I could somehow believe in the manner.

"And her hair," Serena went on. "Such beautiful hair. It was brown with some red in it when she in the sun and she wore it piled up on her head. She had the loveliest clothes, too. It just a pleasure to look at her. In summertime she wore white dresses—not all white, they'd have a little sprig of something against the white. They mostly voile, I think. Sometimes chiffon. I remember one had the print of a pale green fern on it. She always look so cool, so pretty. And her whole soul was just music. You saw her house?"

"Well, not up close, but yes, I saw it."

"I suppose it hard for you to imagine that house, how lovely it was. It was painted white and the lawn always so green and nice. She had a grand piano then and the children used to go hide in the trees and listen while she played. One day she found us out. 'Why, come in,' she said. 'Come in, if you like music that much.' And then she had us to teach her songs and she play with us. She used to come to our church, too, to hear us sing. She say she never had enough and sometimes she say we give her so much pleasure, she like to give some back, and so she'd play for us. Never. I never heard anyone play like she played.

"When her husband taken sick, she say she'd give music lessons then and she had lots of students. But she taken colored, too, for whatever they could pay. When the white people find out she take colored, they say they wouldn't send their children any more unless she refuse colored. She say they stupid to think music had color at all, and she wouldn't refuse anybody who wanted to learn. I think she thought the white people'd give in, but they didn't and pretty soon all her pupils gone. Even the colored then, they thought if they make their children quit maybe the white come back, because this was mostly all she had for her living. But the white people wouldn't. And they cut her children out of things, too, the parties and things like that. So she sent the children away to school. How they torture that woman! The hundreds of ways they think of . . ."

"Was she a northern woman?" I said.

"No," Serena said. "I suppose this surprise you, but she spoke southern. I think that partly why she so sure the white people come around, but I don't know.

"Her husband, he got helpless and they taken him to a naval hospital in Philadelphia. He died there. I was away then, working in that orphanage for several years, and when I came back I didn't recognize Mrs. Emerson. She wasn't as bad as now, but her hair all turn gray and her hands . . . they already shriveled up like that. Some say she hurt them herself, but it look like rheumatism to me. She wasn't out of her mind, then, I don't think. She was still clean. But she used to come to our church to hear the singing. She'd sit in the back and the tears just roll down her face. The choir, they always try to sing her favorites whenever she came. She was very fond of 'Ezekial See the Wheel,' I remember, but to sing while she sat there, never moving, just lettin the tears roll down, it was hard to do. Somebody in the choir nearly always break up. Of course, she'd sold her piano some time ago.

"It just happen slowly a little worse every year. Her clothes wore out and she didn't get new ones. She got so she didn't keep clean. It just about kill me to see that woman dirty, when I think how she was. We thought surely one of her children come soon to take care of her, but they never did. Nobody knows where they are, even. When it's time to pay taxes, Papa he always sees they paid so they don't sell her house away from her."

"Then she really is all alone there," I said. "Nobody takes care of her at all? How does she live?"

"Well, the colored people, you know, after dark, they some- times take food down there and leave it on her porch, but Papa say, 'What's the use to go after dark *now*? Why be careful *now*?

It's too late.' Papa take her food pretty regular right in the day."

"It's no wonder the white people wouldn't answer me when I asked about her," I said. "She must be on their consciences. When I think of how Mr. Tibbs just had the gall to stare at me when I asked him . . ."

"I don't seem to place this Mr. Tibbs you speak of," Serena said.

"Why, the postmaster."

"The *postmaster?*" She sat up in bed and her eyes widened wildly. "Mr. Tibbs the postmaster been dead for ten years!"

I started to laugh. "Well, why don't they take the sign down, then? Oh, I thought I was being so clever, so I wouldn't have to ask his name. You know that sign on the wall that says 'The Post Office of Chinkapink, Montrose County, is hereby classified' and so forth, and then at the bottom the signature of postmaster. Oh, Lord, when I think how six days a week for months, every day I've said 'Good morning, Mr. Tibbs' and he never corrected me, never smiled, just handed me my mail. Why would he do that, Serena?"

"Oh, I don't know," she said. "I guess he think it not worth while to straighten you out, since you're not permanent."

It explained a lot, that remark, and yet I was glad I had asked them all, one at a time, and reminded them about Mrs. Emerson.

"Mrs. Demerest," Serena said, "I want to tell you something. It's about those letters you wrote me in the hospital."

"Yes?"

"Well, you know, I thought and thought how can I ever re-pay such a thing."

"Oh, please, Serena . . ."

"Nobody, in my whole life, nobody ever did such a thing for me. Every day to read the smallest thing about my children, it like they right there in the room with me. You know, when you sick, people ask about your body all the time. They ask about your food. Always they want you to *eat*. But nobody ever try to imagine what on your mind. And that's what matters in a

150

hospital. Now, it too big a thing for me, so I ask God would He repay you for me."

"I'm repaid already."

"No," she said. "I asked God would He give the time, every minute you spent on those letters, would He give it back to you in *inspired* writing time for your own work."

"No more and no less," I said.

"Only what fair," she said.

That night I could hardly wait to tell Ted about Mrs. Emerson, so many frustrated attempts had he been through with me.

"And that's what she said to you first, wasn't it?" Ted said. "Wanting to know if you were one of the ladies of Chinka-pink?"

"Yes. And think of the terrible meaning now of her having said *When they get an idea they're reluctant to part with it.*"

"I suppose," Ted said, "it really is rheumatism?"

"I've seen her hands. I've seen them up close now three times, and I'd swear that it is. And yet there's a kind of truth in that myth they've made. I can see her doing it. I can see her holding up the top of the piano with her head and then stepping back and letting it fall on her hands in an awful fury."

"In five or ten years," Ted said, "I suppose that will be the way that it *was.*"

"The strange thing is," I said, "all the time I've been asking and asking about Mrs. Emerson and never thinking to ask Serena—all the time I had the key to it right here."

"How's that?"

"You know those scraps of paper that Joey practices his typing on? They usually say *Joey Covington* or *roses are red, violets are blue,* and I throw them away when I clean up. Well, there was one, right in the beginning, and it didn't register until now. He wrote *There was once another lady liked colored, but the white people hate her.*"

"It seems so fantastic, all that hatred over a few music lessons," Ted said, "and yet if the white people had some other explanation of the madness, you'd think they'd be quick to volunteer it."

When I told him how Mrs. Covington had asked God to give me back in writing time the amount I had spent on the daily letters to her, he said, "But you didn't keep track, so how will you ever know when you're back on your own time?"

"It's nice that way. Always, whenever it goes well, I can think that I must still be on Serena's time. And, listen, Ted, did I tell you? Serena says it snows here sometimes. Wouldn't it be wonderful if there were snow for Christmas and we could . . ."

"Molly, please don't. Please don't count on Christmas here. Two more men at Special Weapons got warning orders yesterday. It could be my turn now, just any day."

"Oh," I said, "really?" And suddenly the thought of leaving this place lay like a chill on my heart. To leave Serena, the woods, the picnics by the creek? A terrible rush of affection washed out from me over everything in the house, even including Nothing Elaborate and Halfway Decent. Almost, it embraced the Wilkies.

There was frost on the ground now every morning and in the hardware store they got in some Christmas decorations. Feeling as though such an act might penetrate to and influence decisions in the Pentagon, I bought a few decorations because I couldn't resist, and the next day I went back and bought a few more. Joey came, saying he had located running pine in the woods, and Ted and I went with him to find it. There was running cedar, too, and we brought big armfuls of it home and, as Serena had said they did in her childhood, we put it around all the door frames and picture frames. Gradually the spicy odor penetrated everything. All my fancy cookie cutters and my springerle board had been lost in one of our moves, but most of the Christmas recipes were impossible anyway because of the sugar, so all the cookies had to be made of cake mixes.

Serena was up, now, and downstairs, still very thin but looking better. In the afternoons she and I would work on the presents for the children. We were knitting gloves from some yarn she had and making a wool jacket and a new skirt for Sarah. I would do the cutting out and the machine work and Serena would do the hand finishing.

Then, several days before Christmas, when we woke up, we knew there was something strange. The sounds were all different. Ted stood at the window. "Come and look," he said. And there was snow. Deep snow over everything. It was Sunday and we hurried through breakfast and into our warm clothes and out into the snow. At last something had cracked the reserve of the natives and the people we met out were smiling and excited and friendly because it was such a rare thing, this snow, that they forgot we were only temporary and not worth taking the trouble to know. The tiny town with its soft white covering looked like the villages on Christmas cards, the Methodist church steeple now dominating everything. In the years since, I have never been able to see such Christmas cards without thinking, where is the old evil under the snow? Where is the deep distrust? The smoldering hate?

"Oh, but I want to find the moss," I said. "Serena said there was a moss with red flowers that only bloomed under the snow."

"I might as well get an ax," Ted said. "Even if the orders come now, we'd surely have thirty-six hours." So he got the ax and also Joey, so Joey could get a tree, and we started for the high woods. Joey had a sled carefully saved from the time when he had lived in the North. It was too small for him, but it didn't matter. It was a rare treasure to have here and he would bring his tree home on it.

It was the first time for Ted and me to get our own Christmas tree in the woods, and the time of decision was much prolonged. Finally, before we froze, we made the decision (Joey had long ago chosen his and gone home with it). Ted carried the tree over his shoulder. Here, in this unfamiliar part of the woods, we found, like presents spread out for us, the special red-flowered moss and wintergreen, revealed as our feet kicked up the snow.

153

Now that Ted had made this much of a gesture toward Christmas, I no longer felt guilty about my preparations and so we went whole hog and built a crèche out of fagots, split and jointed. (The crèche still serves; in twenty moves afterward, it has never been lost, though replacement of camels has been high and Joseph, poor Joseph, lost his nose before the next Christmas.)

Nothing Elaborate had been cleared for Christmas and on this we set a tray which held the moss with a few pieces of ice kept on it so that it wouldn't dry out in the heat of the house. Part of it served as the manger floor, unorthodox as that was. I produced the decorations and pulled my makeshift cookies out of hiding. Also for the tree I had stuck toothpicks in doughnuts (now hard as rocks) and put cranberries on the ends of the toothpicks. These, too, hung on the tree.

Christmas Eve, bathed and in clean sheets, we lay in bed surrounded with the wonderful odor of pine and cedar, tired from our preparations, knowing the tree in the next room was decorated and present-footed, and by candlelight Ted read the Nativity from St. Luke. I fell asleep thinking it couldn't be more perfect, this unwarlike Christmas, if we knew it to be the last we'd have, which, as it turned out, it was, for a long, long time.

Early Christmas morning Joey came down to invite us to his grandfather's house for the annual eggnog. I closed the oven door on the roasting duck, put on my new Christmas jewelry and we went up. We had never been in the house before.

"Merry Christmas, Captain Demerest," Mr. Loftis said. "Merry Christmas, Mrs. Demerest. I very glad to see you. Every year on Christmas I always have eggnog for all my customers." He ladled us each a cup of the eggnog from a huge cut-glass bowl, and we took ours and stood back to exchange greetings with the others present. There were several white men there, looking very shy, drinking their eggnogs. There were a few colored couples, keeping rather to themselves, also quiet and rather ill at ease. There was no other white woman. Mr. Loftis, however, was magnificently at ease, ladling out eggnog, saying *Merry Christmas* over and over, thanking Miss Addie as she came in from the kitchen to replenish the bowl. Miss Addie nodded gravely in her usual manner and went back into the kitchen again.

It was a wonderfully brave undertaking, one day a year, under the guise of Christmas, the sanction of "custom," all the rightness of a merchant's remembering his customers, that Mr. Loftis actually got a few white people to be served at the same festive bowl with colored people, and I would have given anything to know what was in his head then, ticking off the customers he carried on credit, the ones who never turned down a free drink (the liquor was the best), the attendance as compared with last year's. And when had it come to him, I wondered, the plan of the only possible way this could be accomplished— a man in his own house, in the spirit of Christmas, offering hospitality to anyone who came, but whose guests entered by their own volition? And then the door opened again and there was Taylor Frye.

"Merry Christmas, Mr. Taylor," Mr. Loftis said.

"Merry Christmas, Abel," Taylor said.

Taylor Frye, too, of course, was in business, I thought. And yet it doesn't matter really why he came. And that was what Mr. Loftis knew. Their motivations (and he must have known them all) didn't deny the fact that on one day of the year some colored and some white people entered his house and stood together and drank together and said, because he could make them say it, *Merry Christmas* to one another. And yet if I had charged him with having planned the whole thing to accomplish what could only possibly be accomplished on this one day a year, if I had said to him that I guessed at the pleasure it must be to him to have them thank him ("Thank you, Abel." "Very good eggnog, Abel." "Merry Christmas, Abel"), I felt sure he would have denied any such motivation or knowledge, would have turned on me his best "customer" smile and said he just wanted to wish all his customers Merry Christmas in this way. What he did actually say, as we were leaving, was, "Mrs. Demerest, I always meant to ask you where you from. I don't mean just the last place you stationed, but where you born."

"Kansas," I said.

"Well, well," he said. He looked about the room, checking. So did I. At that moment (it was the dinner hour in Chinka-pink) there were no other white people in the room. "Well, maybe that's it," he said. "Maybe that account for it." He bounced on the balls of his feet, as he did sometimes when he was considering saying something, as he had the day he told me of his worry over Serena. And then, apparently, he changed his mind. The smile left his face. "You a long way from your mamma," he said. "A long way."

Near the end of January, Serena made her last trip to the clinic, the doctor dismissed her, and she began to work half days in the store again. She had regular and reassuring letters from Albert Devereaux and, if he could get leave, they planned to be married sometime around Easter. "But I got to get out of debt," she said. "I can't marry him with debts."

"And we've got to make our trip to the woods," I said. "When do you think you'll be up to it? You know, the paths have ice on them now and you've got to feel surefooted and able to stand the cold."

"I think I'll be ready," she said, "almost any time now. I'm feeling stronger all the time. I wonder could we get as far as the rhododendrons?"

"Where are they?"

"It's pretty far," she said, "and I haven't been there in so long I don't know if they still there. But oh, they used to be so beautiful. They're beyond the old dam. That's what I thought of the most when I was sick. If only I could show you the wild rhododendrons."

156

I had not been that far myself, but I had been as far as the old dam which once had furnished power for the mill. The stone part of the dam was worn away to uselessness, but many of the old logs, slick and rotten, still lay about. The path here had been obliterated, and I knew we would have considerable climbing to do over rough ground. If that was what she had her heart set on, then it was not indicated today or tomorrow. "I tell you," I said, "let's go on Lincoln's birthday. And afterwards we'll come back to my place and have a hot drink and a little quiet celebration."

"All right," she said. "They don't keep his birthday here, I suppose you know. The bank stay open and the post office."

"We'll keep it," I said.

"All right," she said. "If it's freezin or rainin or no matter what, let's go anyway."

13

TED AND I simply held our breaths these days, for he was the only one left unassigned of the group he had come with to Special Weapons. And then finally, about the first of February, he came home with the news. "But it's only an assignment for reassignment," he said. "I'll only be there two weeks, and I have no idea where the appointment will be. It could be right back here, though that's unlikely. It really would be more sensible for me to go alone and for you not to join me until I know where we're going, except for . . ."

"It does sound more sensible," I said. "Except for what?"

He had his head in the hot towel and the steam curled up about it, filling the room with the scent of lemon verbena and witch hazel. He lifted his head and looked about the room, now so pleasant by candlelight, so much our own, so full of history in this little time. "Except for tearing it apart," he said. "All this, alone."

"Believe me," I said, "it wouldn't be any easier for having you witness the destruction."

158

"We'll surely never have such a good place again, so out of things, so private."

Six months ago he had called it grim, and my bringing out the roots box had seemed to him a pathetic gesture. "No," I said, "I'd rather do it alone. With you here to see me agonize over each thing, I'd dissolve in sentimentality. But if you've been away for two weeks, I'll be thinking of joining you." Not to mention, I thought, the two weeks' hotel bill which he might be able to avoid if he were alone. There were often bachelor quarters available on established fields.

"Well, if you can do it, I'd like to walk out of it with it looking just like this. I wish we both could."

"Besides," I said, "we've only got three days. I don't want to spend them packing. I'd rather we had the time together to go to the woods."

So that's the way it was. We went to the woods. We packed Ted's trunk. We went about the town saying good-by and taking pictures and Mrs. Roebuck said John Quincy could have the grocery truck for our last day so that Ted could take his luggage with him, I could see him off, and return with John Quincy.

I didn't feel like talking on the way home and I guess John Quincy knew it.

Lincoln's birthday, as it turned out, was the coldest day in fifty years in that country, but fortunately Serena and I didn't know it. We knew it was cold, all right, but "Nothing," Serena said, "nothing is going to keep me from that trip to the woods, now that I know you got so short a time." I was resigned now to the fact that I would never see Dead Man Hill and never know if my hair would have stood on end.

We were both so bundled up in so many layers of clothing that we looked like two fat dumpies. However, there was no one to see us. We had the entire woods to ourselves. And they were a fantasy. Each smallest twig was coated with ice and it was like walking in a fairyland made of sugar or spun glass. The air was full of crackling sounds, some almost bell-like, and our two columns of breath stood like white candles before us.

The path on which we crept, single file, was covered with ice and we slipped about and half fell and laughed at ourselves until the pain of breathing in the cold air would make us stop. Alternately, we would offer to quit and go home for the sake of the other one, but neither of us wanted to be the one to put an end to it, so we kept on until we came to the old dam. Here there was a remnant of stone wall that must be negotiated and it, too, was covered with ice. What's more, a slip could mean a fall into the water. Though it was not swift here, as it was down lower in the creek, still it was wet and would turn to ice in that air. We went on, awkwardly, cautious as a couple of old cats on a wet floor. Serena was now ahead of me and, as she made a turn on the new path, I heard her let out a groan.

There were the rhododendrons we had come so far to see. They were black, their leaves curled and drooping in the very picture of despair. "Oh, I could cry," she said. "I could just cry."

"Well, we'd really better go back now, I guess," I said, turning away and starting to lead the way back. Whatever possessed her to do it, I don't know, and she said later that she didn't either, but she reached out for two of the poor black things and their stems snapped off with the sound of cracking bones.

When we got back to the house, I had to uncurl her hand to get the flowers loose and my own hands were so numb I could only fumble at the rhododendrons. I put the black things down on the drainboard and started to fill the kettle for coffee. Meanwhile Serena was trying to strike a match to get the fire started in the kerosene stove. In the warmth of the room my nose started to run. My handkerchief was in an inside pocket and I had not even unbuttoned my outer coat yet. Serena handed me her handkerchief and as I blew my nose into it, I knew I would forget about it and throw it into the laundry. I did. For a year or two later, until it wore out, I used to find it in the ironing and remember that day.

Our stiff fingers fumbled at scarves and buttons. We finally got out of the top layer of clothing. Serena had on a little black stocking cap and it had fine ice crystals all over it. I poured rum into the coffee and we sat down at the kitchen table with the oven door open beside us and we wrapped our hands around the cups to feel the warmth. "To Abraham Lincoln!" we said, and drank. Really, then, as our feet slowly came to life and began to tingle and the skin of our ears and noses began to burn, we realized that it *had* been colder than we thought and we *had* done something quite amazing.

"Look!" Serena said, suddenly pointing to the drainboard, and there where we had hurriedly thrown down the black, disappointing things were two beautiful rhododendron blossoms unfurled in full bloom. "And we missed it," she said. "To think we missed it."

"But it couldn't have been anything but the temperature," I said. "Maybe we can duplicate it." So we put them out on the back porch and when they were once again all indrawn and black we brought them in and put them on the table between us. Not to miss it, we quit talking. We sat in silence, drinking the rum-laced coffee, watching the ugly black stalks. Slowly, before our eyes, the two beautiful white blossoms unfolded. And now our nostrils had unfrozen enough that we could smell the sweet, fresh perfume. Over the flowers our eyes met and we smiled. It was not a thing for words.

Next day I began dismantling the house, packing the roots box, the books, the clothes we wore to the woods. Sarah and Joey helped me with washing the woodwork and crating some of the things. They sang while they worked:

> Ezekiel saw the wheel
> Right in the middle of the sky.
> The big wheel runs by power,

But the little wheel runs by the grace of God.
Wheel in wheel in wheel,
Right in the middle of the sky,

and I thought of Mrs. Emerson sitting in the back of the church, the tears silently rolling down her face.

The curtains (or would they be bedspreads in the next place?) were laundered and packed away and I sat in what was no longer our house but Taylor Frye's, returned to its original grimness. Even our ashtrays were packed and I was back with STOLEN FROM 211 by the time the phone call came from Ted. I was to meet him in Chicago, wiring my arrival time when I learned it, and from there we would take a train out to the new place which he couldn't say over the phone. So I went over to Roebuck's to see if I could ride into Hester with John Quincy and to Taylor Frye's to tell him I'd be leaving for sure. Then I went down to say good-by to Mr. Loftis. It wasn't easy. I just put out my hand and he took it in his tremendous one for a moment. "I never forget you and the Captain," he said. "Never."

Joey was in the store and I asked him to tell his mother I was leaving the next day. I wasn't up to saying good-by again at the moment. I hoped Serena would come down in the morning, but if she couldn't I knew John Quincy would let me stop at her house the last thing.

She came, though, walking in quietly, her eyes very red, her whole posture one of studied control. "I know," she said, "how you want to leave everything perfect here. So you have your coffee right up to the time you leave. Then when you gone with John Quincy I'll wash the last cup and saucer and clean out the pot and carry out the grounds to the garbage and take the key over to Mr. Taylor Frye."

"Oh, thank you, Serena. We'll have the last pot together. I guess you know how I hate to leave."

"Don't talk like that," she said. "It taken me two hours to

162

get myself under control to get down here. Don't say anything to get me started cryin. Here, I brought you a plate. It belong to my great-aunt. It's ninety years old."

"Why, Serena," I said, "are you sure you want me to have it? Isn't it valuable now for your family?" For it said on it, in faded gold letters, *Souvenir of Chinkapink*. I thought of the days when Chinkapink had been a resort and "the ladies," as Mr. Loftis had told me, "carried those little parasols."

"I want you to have it," she said. "I know you love the town, even the way it is. And so do I. I'm sorry the plate so brown, though." It had a faded rose in the center above the gold lettering and the outline of a blue border around it. And in a thousand places it was crackled and brown. "You see," she went on, "it just the right size to set on the warming shelf above the stove and not tip over. My great-aunt she always set the hotbread on it to keep it warm because when she called them to dinner, the men, you know, they generally always didn't come. And she taken some of the hotbread and set it on the shelf so it keep warm. There's another plate just like it and it all brown, too. I've got it at home and I think that must be all there are left in the world. At least, I never heard of any others."

I went to pack the plate carefully in the handbag I would keep with me. We had had our coffee in the kitchen, the coffee table having gone with Ted as, once again, his footlocker. Now I called to Serena to come into the living room and sit with me while I was repacking the bag. I saw that she was on the verge of tears again.

"Serena," I said, "you mustn't feel so bad. I'm not dying. I'll write to you, you know. We'll keep in touch always."

"Oh," she said, "I know you mean to *now*. But people go away, they forget. Time and distance, they . . ."

"No," I said. "No, I don't forget, Serena. I do write to my friends. You and I, we've been too close. We've been such friends, how can you think I would forget you?"

163

"Oh, I know you mean to now. But the war and all, and nobody ever came back to Chinkapink."

"You did," I said.

"Yes," she said, "I did. Well, anyhow, I've got to quit thinkin about myself. The children gave me all kinds of messages for you. They afraid to come today. I would have let them stay home from school, but they said they knew they'd cry and make things terrible. And then there's so many messages from all the colored. My land, I was up till midnight last night, one after another comin in. They all want me to tell you how . . . how much they miss you, how they hope everything go fine for you and the Captain."

"Well, how *nice*," I said, "but I must say I'm surprised."

"Why? Why should you be?"

"Well, because," I said, "they hardly know me. I would like to have known more of the colored people, but you're the only ones, you and the children and your father, that I really got to know."

"They know *you*," she said.

"Oh, no, Serena. I wish they did, but most of them can't even recognize me. Why, it hasn't been two days since I spoke to Leora Rochelle in the postoffice and she didn't know me from Adam. I always speak to Fedora, too, and she never knows me, either."

Serena was very agitated. She seemed almost angry. "I can't let you think that," she said. "I can't let you go away from here thinkin they don't even know you, when they know the smallest thing about you. How you have candles on the dinner table and where you go to write on your book in the woods by the persimmon tree. They see you never disturbed there. And that time you were so late from shopping and the Captain got his own dinner and washed the dishes *with his hat on*. They still talking about that. Why, they know . . . they know . . ." She spoke so rapidly now in her agitation, that I couldn't get a word in. "Why, even your laundry that you send into Fort Lassiter.

There's a girl from here works in the Fort laundry and she see that your laundry always taken care of in a special way. She know even your tablecloths by heart. Week before last, she mend a hole in that blue one herself."

"But Serena," I said. "I can hardly believe this. If they know all that about me, if they take such pains, why in God's name don't they *speak* to me?"

"Why, they was protectin you," she said.

"*What?*"

"Protectin you," she said. "Always."

I sat back in my chair and just stared at her. And now, suddenly, I could believe it. For sometimes I did meet one of them in the alley, and in memory I could hear the greeting, *Good evenin, Mrs. Demerest*, not just *evenin*, as any stranger, white or black, might greet another.

"The idea," I said, "it's just so . . ."

"Oh, yes," Serena said, "you hadn't been here but a couple of weeks before we all had a meetin in the church. Papa, he talked. It was a regular prayer meetin night so nobody would think anything different at a big meetin. We sang some songs and the minister he prayed. You know, if only the colored sing spirituals, then nobody pay any mind. They go on by. Papa, he never very strong for religion, like some, you know, but he let it be known he'd be there. I guess the minister pretty surprised such a big attendance at prayer meetin on Wednesday night. It mostly the old ladies come on Wednesday night. But the church full that night. And then Papa, at the end, he ask the minister if he could say something. And so Papa got up.

"Papa never shout. He just talk quiet, but when Papa say he *mean* something, you listen. He look at them. I remember it so well. And he wait for them to be quiet. You know, Papa he so *big*, really, and when he on a platform, they listen. And Papa, he say, 'All right, now you got another one like Mrs. Emerson. *This* time, take care of her. *This* time you got the husband, too, so you gotta be twice as careful. Watch yourself.

In the day. In the night. Watch yourselves and be careful of them.' "

"My God," I said. And I might have left here, not knowing, I thought. Now a hundred events started whirling through my memory, all topsy-turvy in their need for reconstruction. What did I know that I thought I knew? What was I taking of their town that I thought mine to take? Was there anything, the slightest event, that didn't now have to be reinterpreted? "Serena," I said, "Serena, they did it too well. I didn't have an inkling. I didn't understand." And now I would have asked a thousand questions. How about Benedict in jail? How about . . .

But John Quincy was at the kitchen door saying it was time to go. Serena got up immediately. "Don't worry," she said. "I'll wash the cups. I'll wipe the table. I'll empty the ashtray. I'll do everything just the way you would."

She and John Quincy carried the bags out to the truck while I put on my coat and hat. Still stunned from the revelation she had given me, I looked back at the rooms where Ted and I had had our best home (and the best we would have until long after the war was over), but the loss didn't really penetrate then. I kissed Serena good-by and got into the truck. I had nothing whatever to say. John Quincy got in behind the wheel beside me and closed his door.

"God keep you," Serena said. "God keep you and the Captain in the holder of His hand."

And then John Quincy started the truck, Serena put up her hand to wave and, as long as I could keep the house in sight, she was still standing there with no coat on in the icy wind, her hand still waving.

"You know," John Quincy said, "that woman, she pure goodness. Just goodness."

I bent my head into my hands and burst into tears. John Quincy said nothing, just drove steadily on. When the truck stopped, he got out and unloaded all the luggage and carried it into the station, leaving me alone to get my face mended, my nose blown, my hat adjusted, my gloves located.

"Where you gone meet the Captain?" he said.

"Chicago."

"Oh, yes," he said. "Chicago."

"Have you been there?" I asked, for suddenly a look of such longing had come over his face.

"No, ma'am," he said. "But I heard about it."

I suppose he put me on the train. Somebody must have. I have a dim memory of winding through some mountains and some time later became aware that we had stopped at Knoxville in Tennessee. I was still in a state of shock. It is not easy to find one has been fighting the good fight from a downy bassinette. They had *hovered* (they had instructed their children to hover) over me, who had since childhood embraced battles as though they were long-stemmed roses from a lover. Me, a born defender, *defended?* Me, the protector, *protected?* Me?

I couldn't get over it. I kept thinking of things in this new light. I felt their terrible anxiety (*Watch yourself. In the day. In the night.*) that before their eyes I might turn into Mrs. Emerson.

I had not read the last mail, having tossed it into my bag, and now I got it out to read, hoping there would be something, some letter from somebody *who knew who I was,* that would get me oriented and out of this stunned condition. But the very first letter I opened was from the college where I had written to inquire about Sarah's chances of entrance.

Dear Mrs. Demerest,
    We regret . . . the Montrose school . . . not accredited . . .

So now there would come the testing of Serena's gamble—whether it is better to live in a house you own near the presence f a respected grandfather or get an education with your mamma away from home, an education and a chance for a better job. I folded the letter and put it away. Later, later. Not just now.

The train was four hours late getting into Chicago and, since most trains were late in the war years, we had arranged that I should go to the coffee shop and that Ted would report there as often as he could. I sank down tiredly on a stool at the counter and saw with a shock that the man next to me was colored. *Oh, God, there'll be a scene and I'm so tired, so tired.* But the waitress was also colored and she took his order and then mine and suddenly I realized where I was. I was *out.*

"You look mighty tired," the waitress said.

"I am," I said. The man next to me was reading a magazine. There was nothing between him and the waitress, no secret accord, no leaguing against me, or about me, or even for me. He was, simply, as I was, a traveler and a customer. The waitress was to him exactly as she was to me, a stranger. And suddenly I remembered the longing on John Quincy's face as he had said, "Chicago. I heard about it."

Then Ted was there, saying we had only fifteen minutes to make the train and where was my baggage check? And so we were running, running, all over the place and down a long ramp and onto the train and finally we sat there together, just breathing, just letting our hearts pound. "Where are we going?" I said, and he showed me the tickets. "But that's . . ." It was an embarkation center, I knew.

"Yes," Ted said. "It'll be pretty soon now, but we'll have a little time together and a long, long train ride. Let's go into the diner. Let's not talk about it until after dinner. I haven't had anything to eat since breakfast. Have you?"

"I don't think so. I don't remember."

After we had stood in line in the diner for a long time we finally sat down and ordered. "Well, tell me the news from home," he said. "Was it too terrible taking it all apart? And Mrs. Covington, did she see you off?"

"Yes. Oh, Ted, it wasn't the way we thought. It was all, all that time . . . they were . . ."

168

"Why, Molly, what is it? What happened? I saw the way you looked, but I thought you were just tired and hungry."

"Well, probably I am," I said. "I shouldn't try to tell you here, it's so sad."

"All right," he said. "Let's wait. Let's have dinner first. Mrs. Covington isn't sick again, or Mr. Loftis—nothing's happened to Mr. Loftis?"

"Oh, no," I said. "It's nothing like that at all. It's really, I suppose, very funny, in a way."

"Only you don't seem to see the humor of whatever it is," he said.

"No, it's too soon."

Well, there was his news, which we couldn't discuss in public, and there was mine, which I didn't think I could tell without tears. And so we put them both aside the best we could. We were together after an absence. And we were hungry. Finally Ted remembered that he had run into people we had known at an earlier station and that carried us through. But settled down again in our seats, seeing the lights come on in the little towns, the sadness of all trains came back to remind me as one state of detachment calls to another, and so at last I told him, told him how I had been "protected," how Mr. Loftis had spoken at the prayer meeting.

"To think," I said, "all that time, while I blundered on and on, they were hovering around. All that time, and I didn't know. I never even felt it."

"Well," Ted said, "I guess we can take some pride in the fact it took a hundred of them to do it, working day and night. At least we gave them the satisfaction of knowing they did a sizable job."

But it didn't help me. It was too soon. I knew in time I'd see the irony of it, but just now all I could do was stare out the window at the darkness and try not to dissolve in helpless weeping.

"But Ted," I said, suddenly turning to him. "If their enemies

169

won't help them, and if they daren't *let* their friends help them, then . . . then how . . . ?"

"Well," he said, "I suppose they figure to do it for themselves."

My hand in his, I sat quietly, trying to accept this thing (Was it only this morning? No, it had been yesterday) and digest it, so that I could be out of Chinkapink and turning to *us, our news,* the little time that we might have left.

"But you must remember," Ted said, touching my arm so that I would turn to him. "You must remember that Lee Carter Higgins has no children and Serena has. Lee Carter will die, in time."

"But the Wilkies have children."

"Gary Cooper, you mean? What will Gary Cooper be able to do on marshmallows and chocolate when Joey's grandfather has his hands on wholesale meat?"

And his mother goes on and on with patent medicines, I thought, while Serena does what is necessary to stay alive.

And then, at last, I saw the extra bar. "Why, Captain," I said, "you're a captain."

"It took you long enough to notice."

"You know," I said, "Serena doesn't believe me. It's so sad. She doesn't really believe that I'll remember her, or write to her."

"She doesn't know you, surely," he said.

"She thinks I mean to, all right. It's just that time and distance make things different, she thinks."

"Well, then, you know something she doesn't, don't you?"

"Yes," I said. "Now *I* know something that will surprise *her.*"

And so we laughed together, and it would be all right now. I would not be lost in some past puzzlement in Chinkapink when we needed to be alive to each other in this little, shrinking present.

"Do you know what she said to me, Ted, the very last thing, when she was standing by the truck?"

170

"Serena?"

"Yes. She said, 'God keep you. God keep you and the Captain in the holder of His hand.' "

"Sounds like a good place," he said. "Good place to be."

I thought of it, longingly, as though it might be a physical place, the holder of His hand, and the two of us safe inside there. Who was it now? (Sometimes I got them so mixed up, God and Mr. Loftis.) Had it been Mr. Loftis or God who had stood so baffled, staring out into space, saying "How can it *be*? How can it be that little children cry theirselves to sleep in a man's own house and him not *know*?"

THE END

MY DEAR MRS. DEMEREST,

I received your letter. I was just so glad to hear from you. Just no words to express the joy I derived from it. Joey very happy over the books you sent him and I think that big one be a big help to him. They don't seem to teach geography in his school any more.

Did I tell you about our garden? We have potatoes, tomatoes up, string beans, okra, cabbage still just plants. Joey and I are very proud of it. A man came in the store, told me he saw Joey swim across Chinkapink Creek yesterday. I am glad he has learned because he loves to fish. Now I feel better satisfied when he does go. Sarah is cutting her wisdom tooth. She is getting some shape now, beginning to look grown up.

My brother John over seas now. Papa send his best regards to you and Lieutenant Demerest.

Last Friday night the phone rang. I answered to my great surprise it was Albert. Saying Hello dear, I am in your home state. Then you can just imagine how thrilled I was. Nice to know he is this near even if I couldn't say much of what I felt there in the store with the customers and all. I see in the papers they are there on maneuvers. I never knew they allowed them to tell such things.

May God keep you in the Holder of His hand.

Yours sincerely,

SERENA

February 18, 1944

DEAR MRS. DEMEREST,

I received your good letter and it made me so glad. You know Mrs. Demerest there are times when your heart bubble up and your eyes brim over and no words you can find to express how you feel. Albert had a five-day furlough. He was here two days. Not time enough to get married. He surprised me as I was not looking for him. Has been promoted to corp.

Sarah is so anxious to go in training for a nurse since she can't get in the college. I want to take her up to Lincoln Hospital thinking if they saw her size they just might let her in. She is seventeen her next birthday. Suppose to be eighteen. They have the cadet school of nursing there. Also she has written Harlem Hospital in New York. The thing about Lincoln is that she could live with my grandmother there and it would help a lot on the expense.

You know the house you lived in when you were here got burned down. Mr. Taylor Frye say damaged to the extent of $2000. But all your places in the woods just the same and the fireplace Lieutenant Demerest built it still there.

Papa send his best regards to you both.

Respectfully,

SERENA

MY VERY DEAR MRS. DEMEREST,

It is very pretty here now. The violets and jonquils, forsythia, bridlewreath, hyacinth all in bloom.

Joey has been cleaning up the yard. Planted seven cedar trees from the corner of the house to the next door fence. He also made a fence by taking some wire the linesman gave John when they put the extra lines through here and he had saved it for clothesline. We run it from the house to the post and then back till we got it the height we wanted. Maybe we will plant a vine to grow on it. Then we planted barberry bushes. Then Joey put a row of bricks. Then a little further we planted a hawthorn bush with a ring of brick around it. Around the bush Joey planted tulips violets and jonquils. Then a spice bush Joey found in the wood bloom yellow in the spring, very tiny blossom. Then we have a bench to sit on.

Albert now on the other side.

Joey has been very anxious to go to Fort Lassiter to work. He got a job as dishwasher but he will have to stay nights. His bed going to be right next to a man from here. Him and Papa were boys together. So I have consented for him to try it. Oh no not for a minute do I think he will stay any length of time but it will prepare him for the next job he undertakes.

When you write your husband please tell him I would like to pay my respects to him. He is still in my daily prayers. Papa always say of him he was a man among men.

Sincerely,

SERENA

DEAR MRS. DEMEREST,

I do hope with all my heart you have heard from Captain Demerest by now. Alberts letters are very slow in coming too. I have not heard from him for a month now.

Sarah is now trying to get her papers filled out application paper for St. Luke's Hospital in Charleston. Her school principal has filled out his part. Doctor's papers are fixed up now. The dentist is holding us up because we could not get an appointment until today. She has six teeth to be filled.

The wild honeysuckle just about choked up your old path in the woods. My how it smells. You can smell it clear up at the post office.

Joey so tall now you wouldn't know him. All the boys went across Chinkapink Creek to play ball. Joey just came in tell me they got beat. The other boys had more practice than they had. Ha ha some excuse.

Well my dear I will close now.

Yours sincerely,

SERENA

February 4, 1945

MY VERY DEAR MRS. DEMEREST,

Let me thank you very much for the snapshots. When I saw that picture of you and your dog tears of joy streamed down my face. I felt as though you were right here. Joey taken some pictures with his camera. As soon as they are developed I'll send you some. Joey has a job as helper on a coal truck and he likes it.

I received notice saying Albert Devereaux was wounded in action. I do hope and pray this war will soon be over. It is very cold here now. They have been skating for two weeks on the river. I do wish I could paint the river with all the skaters and their many pretty colors and the graceful skating.

Sarah's age was against her at the hospital and she did not get in the cadet training. It was a bad disappointment for her. They wrote and advised her to go to college and take five subjects which will help her later. But of course you know her high school not accredited so she can't get into college either. She found out she could go to night school at Howard University, so I let her go to stay with an aunt of Papa's in Washington D.C. First she worked in a restaurant days and went to night school, but they said she wanted to enroll in too much and so she can only take one course. She is taking chemistry. She taken a Civil Service examination to be a messenger and passed it, so now she works in the Pentagon days and take her chemistry at night. I'm more than sorry to say Joey does not want to go on to school.

I received the purple heart from Albert Devereaux.

Mr. Roebuck sold out his store to Piggly Wiggly. My brother John still in the South Pacific. Papa been having some rheumatism this winter but otherwise he seem well. He send his best regards to you. I will close now.

Devotedly,

SERENA

176

My very dear Mrs. Demerest,

Today is VE Day which brings me memories of you. I do hope you and the Captain will be together real soon. As I sit looking out over the river it look so calm and serene from here. It brings peace and comfort to me. Here there is no excitement however we are all thankful to God.

I haven't heard from Albert for nearly four months now. I see by the Afro the company still in Italy, but their outfit had been broken up and they had been put in other outfits so I decided its no use to write till I hear from him. I had been writing every Sunday night and maybe Wednesday.

I am so happy for you you finish your book you been working on so long. You always impress me as one person who would do what she started out to do. I remember once you said you could write it with a toothbrush if you had to and I believe you could. I feel sure it is a book that will touch a lot of people and I pray you have a big success with it.

I do hope Captain Demerest gets home soon.

Sincerely,

Serena

DEAR MOLLY,

Well you say surely by now can't I bring myself to call you Molly as long as we been friends and getting through the war and all. I guess I was just waiting for you to ask.

We spent a lovely Christmas here even though it was very bad outside sleet rain and hail. The ground was like glass. But I was very busy inside and did not go out till night. I had the Family for Dinner so you see I was very busy cooking and different ones coming in all day. Of course Papa had the egg nog at his place the same as always in the morning. You know I do believe it was the most joyous I have had in a long time. Brother John and Albert Devereaux both here. John's girl came from New York, also my sister Evelyn. Was eleven for dinner. I cooked turkey the first time since I've been in my little house here. I just can't explain to you the joy it was yet. Albert working in Lawtonville and comes down weekends. We to be married in two weeks. He still very handsome for to have been shot in the face.

Joey brought home a spray of rhododendron it brought tears to my eyes as it was all folded back. Then it came up like it did that last time we were together. It brought back such sweet remembrance of you.

Papa sends his best regards to you and Captain Demerest. No changes have been made in old Chinkapink.

May God keep you in the Holder of His Hand.

Love,

SERENA

DEAR MOLLY,

You remember Miss Addie I'm sure. My stepmother. Well she had not been feeling well since Xmas. I was taking her for a walk every morning. She was getting weaker all the time. Papa and I carried her into the Clinic at Lawtonville for a K & G test then chest X-ray and blood test. She always had an older doctor before. This time he was not there. Was a young doctor. He asked her how long had she had this heart trouble. I think that did it. She kept telling us something was wrong with her we were not telling her but we knew no more than what the old doctor had told her it was just her nerves.

Came home that night. She made the trip pretty good although she was all in that night when she got home. Next morning Papa ask her how she felt. She did not feel at all good. Said she would get up later. So Papa ask if she want him to help her get dressed. She said no. So Papa said breakfast is ready. I will eat and as soon as Serena comes I will send her up to dress you. I often did that as she would wait for me to fix her meals.

Papa no sooner than started eating breakfast when he heard a shot. She had shot herself. Died in about eight or ten minutes. She was not conscious so we know she did not suffer.

We do not know where she got the strength and regret one of us not up there with her but maybe that the way it supposed to be. Papa's regret was that the old gun was in the dresser drawer. Was one a fellow gave him to keep for him eighteen years ago. You know how careful Papa always was of somebody else's things. Of course we close the store the day of the funeral but next day Papa went to work. John and I didn't try to argue with him. The store his life.

Well, I will close now.

Sincerely,

SERENA

Dear Molly,

Received your good letter with the pictures of your new house. The Captain look very fine. He look different not to be in uniform but otherwise just the way I remember him. This leaves us all well. Papa's rheumatism was bad this winter but now with the warm weather he seem much better. It has been very warm here. I had string beans up 3 or 4 inches. One night the frost came along whoop they all gone. Some people had corn up. I had two peach trees bloomed this year for the first time. You know me. I am still hoping they are going to be all right.

My land I am just so thrilled for you that your book going to be publish. I know it mean so much to you. Just no words to say how I feel for you about it.

You know Molly, there something I want you to know. Albert and I are very happy. I had no idea such happiness was for us or in store for me. God has blessed me in so many ways. Albert has a job much closer home now.

Sarah finally got to start her nursing course. Its much less money for her than her messenger job, but I think she did right. It what she always wanted. Joey and Sarah now both staying with Papa's aunt in Washington D.C. Joey has a job as elevator operator. He like it all right, but he want to go in the Army as soon as they take him. He is taller than Papa now.

Albert send his greetings to you and your husband.

As ever,

Serena

DEAREST MOLLY,

This my morning to open up the store. We taken turns, John Papa and I. I enjoy it really to get the stove going and see the sun come up all alone when everything so quiet. I generally bring over my Bible and read a psalm while waiting for the fire to catch. There are some, the sound of them make me warm inside like "I will lift up mine eyes unto the Hills from whence cometh my help. My help cometh from the Lord which made heaven and earth." That the 121st and then I always love the 28th "The Lord is my strength and my shield; my heart trusted in him and I am helped. Therefore my heart greatly rejoyceth: and with my song will I praise him."

Business is rotten in the store. They are still working on the Dam. I don't know if I told you about the new Dam. Up above the bridge about even with your and Captain Demerest favorite spot, they have built another bridge. They say its to carry equipment across on. I haven't been up there for some time. You have not been allowed while they are working on it. They are doing away with the old reservoir in fact it is up for sale. Was in the paper two weeks ago. I do hope before to long I will be able to get some pictures of it for you. They made a road where your path was.

This leaves us all well. Sarah still in her nursing course. Joey still operating the elevator.

May God guide you and infold you in His care.

Sincerely,

SERENA

January 1, 1949

My Very Dear Molly,

Happy New Year. Joyous New Year to you and your husband. I opened your present Christmas morning. What joy when I found it was your book publish at last. It was a thrill that seem to come from my stomach up into my mouth but stayed in my throat. Couldn't get my breath. I was yelling hurray and thanking God for his Goodness to us and His guidance in all your work. And then the tears came. Albert thought I lost my mind, I just got so excited.

We had such a good Christmas here, so quiet and joyous and peaceful. Papa had his eggnog same as always and then Albert and I had dinner for all the relatives. Was twelve here. Sarah and Joey both home, too. Sarah still in her nursing course. For a while she was engage but she broke it. Joey still want to go in the Army when he old enough.

Yours sincerely,

Serena

P.S. I have started the Book and it surprise me that it sound just the way you talk.

March 21, 1949

DEAREST MOLLY,

I do hope and pray this will find you and Captain Demerest well. We lost Papa Monday at 6:15 A.M. Was buried Wednesday at one o'clock. Monday he was in the store. Tuesday wasn't feeling so good and did not come over but he did not go to bed until Wednesday still thinking he would get up next day. Thursday we had the doctor. He said he had flu. Next day Papa very sick and we carried him to the Hospital in Lawtonville. I stayed till nine o'clock that night. On Sunday when I went up he was unconscious so he did not suffer. Kidney poison it was.

John and I are going to try to carry the business on, if God is willing.

The store so much Papa.

Yours truly,

SERENA

September 7, 1950

DEAREST MOLLY,

I'm sorry its been so long since your good letter came. I've been sick and keep putting off writing. Don't worry about me I feel better now. It was some kind of anemia. I didn't feel so bad, just no pep. At the Clinic they gave me some liver shots and I'm on a diet now. Feeling much better. Papa always say he rather wear out than rust out and since I had this anemia I know what he meant. My dahlias no good this year. The beetles something terrible. I generally go around night and morning with a can of kerosene and pick off the beetles and drop them in, but I didn't feel like it this year and the beetles just took them. Albert tried to do something about my other flowers I planted but he can't tell a weed from a flower and he just pull up everything in sight.

You ask about Sarah's nursing course. Yes she finish it. She had some jobs in private homes but of course there some time between jobs, so she taken a job as nurse in a theater. They call it nurse, but Sarah pretty disgusted with it. In four months she only had two people to faint on her and the usherettes taken all the aspirin.

I keep writing about everything except what I meant. Just so hard to find words to say about you maybe writing a book about Papa and me like you said. You say how would I feel about it and I been trying to think how to say how I feel for weeks now. I guess it like the time of the eclipse here some years back. I was in the store and suddenly everything got so dark I went to the door to see what was the matter. By the time I realize what it was I notice my clothes nearly been torn off me by Delia's two little girls hanging on me so tight. Delia Clarence Rochelle's cousin I don't know if you knew her. Well then it start to get light again and I said my land Children, let loose my dress and I tell them it just an eclipse of the sun. They said they thought it was the end of the world and they knew for sure I'd go to

184

Heaven and they think to hold tight to my skirt so they get in by mistake.

Why Children you mustn't think that of me, I said, and it touch me so I start to cry. I guess that how I feel about you writing a book about Papa and me and all that you said. I just feel so humble.

As ever,

SERENA

May 5, 1951

DEAR MOLLY,

I hope this find you and Captain Demerest well. My flowers are lovely this year. Rains came just right and everything in bloom. My lilac bushes just loaded and smell all through the house. We put in frozen foods in the store. Seem like people just had to have them. I know you thinking where in the world we find the space because the only space left was the middle of the floor. So that's where we put them.

Joey is in Camp Breckenridge. He likes the Army very much and is very good to write. All his letters typewritten now. And it seem to me his spelling improve almost over night.

Well Sarah is engaged. She and her young man came down to see us last weekend. He seems very nice and Albert liked him. He has a good job and Sarah look very happy. They plan to get married in about six months, or sooner if they can find an apartment. Rents are very high and apartments hard to find. Sarah and Joey they both tell me to send their regards to you when I write.

I pray you and the Captain keep in good health.

As ever,

SERENA

January 15, 1952

MY DEAREST MOLLY,

Well now I'm pleased I sent the calendar. I thought maybe you might like to have one. We send them to all the customers. It seem strange to think of it hanging in your kitchen so far away in California. Yes, we kept Papa's name the same. The store still Abel Loftis and Sons. I know you would approve of that. Several people ask John about it, if he going to change the name and John always tell them its the name holding the store together and if ever anybody go to paint over the sign he feel the store fall apart.

Sarah going to be married next month. I think I will go to Washington, D.C. for the wedding. My great aunt that Sarah been living with is 100 years old. Of course her daughter there to help and I don't know how many cousins and William (that Sarahs young mans name) his parents live there, but Albert said it been so many years since I had a vacation and I never will have such a good excuse again. I guess the store will get along somehow without me for a week.

I'll write you all about the wedding. Sarah have such very strong ideas just how everything should be.

Sincerely,

SERENA

My dear Molly,

I guess by now Sarah sent you her wedding pictures. The wedding really very lovely. Sarah wore a white ballerina style dress with a short veil, white lace gloves, white pumps. William black trousers, white coat and shirt, maroon tie, cummerbund and boutonniere. Matron of honor lavender, one bridesmaid in pink and one in yellow. I bought a new dress myself. My land, it been so long since I bought a dress didn't even know my size. I took a 14. My clothes must have been hanging on me without I even notice it. Nicest thing of all Joey got leave from camp and was there to give Sarah away. Joey over six feet. He said to tell you he writes on a typewriter every day now. He does like the Army fine and they send him to special schools. All of a sudden he seem to be very studious and all grown up. But when he had to go I went with him to the station and all the way he held my hand just like when he was little.

Well to get back to the wedding it really was lovely. You know my greataunt still up and about and spry as everything at 100 years of age. We had the reception in her house after the wedding in Church. Little sandwiches, all different shapes, mints, nuts, cookies, punch, different kinds of cake and ice cream. We serve until 11 that night. And then people kept coming in to see Sarah's presents and different relatives that couldn't come to the wedding. We were still serving by Tuesday and we hadn't run out of ice cream yet.

Sarah and William didn't go on a honeymoon trip. They just so happy finally to find a place to live they went to their apartment. It is quite nice, living room, bedroom, bath, kitchen, but far out. One present Sarah got was a green lamp with a shade the exact same color as her living room rug. All her presents very nice, but she and William really thrilled to death over the one from you and the Captain.

I feel quite content in my heart over Sarah. Her husband very

nice boy, quiet and serious, and his people seem solid. I feel like
I been gone a month. Albert say the way I look at everything
What you think going to be changed in a week?

Love,

SERENA

DEAREST MOLLY,

I received your wonderful letter. You sound so joyous. You ask me to write you how the people look in the store on the 18th of May, the day of the Supreme Court Decision and tell you if they smiling, how they walk and hold their heads and what they say before I forget. Theres nothing to forget. The 18th was just another day to us. We have longed so long for equal education so our people can get decent jobs. But next September everything will be just the same that's what everybody knows, no matter what the Supreme Court say. The years go on and the children grow up and their children grow up and always it just the same.

Maybe if Papa was alive, he might have been the way you were thinking of in your letter, I don't know. Of course he would have heard it on the radio and read it in the paper and then later when the Afro came. Maybe Papa would have smiled and walked springy the way he had. But Papa had the long hope. He was not like most.

I'm sorry theres nothing to tell. I know you be disappointed. This leaves us all well. Albert sends greetings to you and the Captain. I will try to write more next time.

As ever,

SERENA

This is a true story. Its people are real, its incidents actually occurred as they have been set down here. Only the names of people and places have been disguised to protect those involved.

If there is no Southern town named Chinkapink, there is at least one like it, sharing its charms, its attitudes and its problems. I know, for I have lived there, and I have known Taylor Frye, Mrs. Emerson, Lee Carter Higgins, and all the others, including, God bless them, Serena and Abel Loftis. Their story has haunted me for many years, and I have written it down for no other reason than to share it with others. In the essential issues there have been no changes in Chinkapink since the date of Serena's last letter. However, our correspondence and our friendship continue to the present moment.

MOLLY DEMEREST